Discoveries & Other Works by W. B. Yeats

William Butler Yeats (1865 – 1939) is best described as Ireland's national poet in addition to being one of the major twentieth-century literary figures of the English tongue. To many literary critics, Yeats represents the 'Romantic poet of modernism,' which is quite revealing about his extraordinary style that combines between the outward emphasis on the expression of emotions and the extensive use of symbolism, imagery and allusions. Yeats also wrote prose and drama and established himself as the spokesman of the Irish cause. His fame was greatly boosted mainly after he received the Nobel Prize in Literature in 1923. His life was marked by his many love stories, by his great interest in oriental mysticism and occultism as well as by political engagement since he served as an Irish senator for two terms. Today, although William Butler Yeats's contribution to literary modernism and to Irish nationalism remains incontestable.

Here we publish a collection of his essays that allow his intellect to roam across many subjects with his analysis, imagery and thoughts creating a spell binding series of works.

Index Of Contents

POETRY AND TRADITION

PREFACE TO THE FIRST EDITION OF JOHN M. SYNGE'S POEMS AND TRANSLATIONS

J. M. SYNGE AND THE IRELAND OF HIS TIME
THE TRAGIC THEATRE
JOHN SHAWE-TAYLOR
EDMUND SPENSER

W. B. Yeats – A Short Biography

PREFACE

When I wrote the essay on Edmund Spenser the company of Irish players who have now their stage at the Abbey Theatre in Dublin had been founded, but gave as yet few performances in a twelve month. I could let my thought stray where it would, and even give a couple of summers to The Faerie Queene; while for some ten years now I have written little verse and no prose that did not arise out of some need of those players or some thought suggested by their work, or was written in the defence of some friend whose life has been a part of the movement of events which is creating a new Ireland unintelligible to an old Ireland that watches with anger or indifference. The detailed defence of plays and players, published originally in Samhain, the occasional periodical of the theatre, and now making some three hundred pages of Mr. Bullen's collected edition of my writings, is not here, but for the most part an exposition of principles, whether suggested by my own work or by the death of friend or fellow-worker, that, intended for no great public, has been printed and published from a Hand Press which my sisters manage at Dundrum with the help of the village girls. I have been busy with a single art, that of the theatre, of a small, unpopular theatre; and this art may well seem to practical men, busy with some programme of industrial or political regeneration, of no more account than the shaping of an agate; and yet in the shaping of an agate, whether in the cutting or the making of the design, one discovers, if one have a speculative mind, thoughts that seem important and principles that may be applied to life itself, and certainly if one does not believe so, one is but a poor cutter of so hard a stone.

W. B. YEATS.
August, 1912.

THOUGHTS ON LADY GREGORY'S TRANSLATIONS

I

CUCHULAIN AND HIS CYCLE

The Church when it was most powerful taught learned and unlearned to climb, as it were, to the great moral realities through hierarchies of Cherubim and Seraphim, through clouds of Saints and Angels who had all their precise duties and privileges. The story-tellers of Ireland, perhaps of every primitive country, imagined as fine a fellowship, only it was to the æsthetic realities they would have had us climb. They created for learned and unlearned alike, a communion of heroes, a cloud of stalwart witnesses; but because they were as much excited as a monk over his prayers, they did not think sufficiently about the shape of the poem and the story. We have to get a little weary or a little distrustful of our subject, perhaps, before we can lie awake thinking how to make the most of it. They were more anxious to describe energetic characters, and to invent beautiful stories, than to express themselves with perfect dramatic logic or in perfectly-ordered words. They shared their characters and their stories, their very images, with one another, and handed them down from generation to generation; for nobody, even when he had added some new trait, or some new incident, thought of claiming for himself what so obviously lived its own merry or mournful life. The maker of images or worker in mosaic who first put Christ upon a cross would have as soon claimed as his own a thought which was perhaps put into his mind by Christ himself. The Irish poets had also, it may be, what seemed a supernatural sanction, for a chief poet had to understand not only innumerable kinds of poetry, but how to keep himself for nine days in a trance. Surely they believed or half believed in the historical reality of even their wildest imaginations. And so soon as Christianity made their hearers desire a chronology that would run side by side with that of the Bible, they delighted in arranging their Kings and Queens, the shadows of forgotten mythologies, in long lines that ascended to Adam and his Garden. Those who listened to them must have felt as if the living were like rabbits digging their burrows under walls that had been built by Gods and Giants, or like swallows building their nests in the stone mouths of immense images, carved by nobody knows who. It is no wonder that one sometimes hears about men who saw in a vision ivy-leaves that were greater than shields, and blackbirds whose thighs were like the thighs of oxen. The fruit of all those stories, unless indeed the finest activities of the mind are but a pastime, is the quick intelligence, the abundant imagination, the courtly manners of the Irish country-people.

William Morris came to Dublin when I was a boy, and I had some talk with him about these old stories. He had intended to lecture upon them, but 'the ladies and gentlemen',he put a communistic fervour of hatred into the phrase,knew nothing about them. He spoke of the Irish account of the battle of Clontarf and of the Norse account, and said, that one saw the Norse and Irish tempers in the two accounts. The Norseman was interested in the way things are done, but the Irishman turned aside, evidently well pleased to be out of so dull a business, to describe beautiful supernatural events. He was thinking, I suppose, of the young man who came from Aoibhill of the Grey Rock, giving up immortal love and youth, that he might fight and die by Murrough's side. He said that the Norseman had the dramatic temper, and the Irishman had the lyrical. I think I should have said with Professor Ker, epical and romantic rather than dramatic and lyrical, but his words, which have so great an authority, mark the distinction very well, and not only between Irish and Norse, but between Irish and other un-Celtic literatures. The Irish story-teller could not interest himself with an unbroken interest in the way men like himself burned a house, or won wives no more wonderful than themselves. His mind constantly escaped out of daily circumstance, as a bough that has been held down by a weak hand suddenly straightens itself out. His imagination was always running to Tir-nan-og, to the Land of Promise, which is as near to the country-people of to-day as it was to Cuchulain and his companions. His belief in its nearness, cherished in its turn the lyrical temper, which is always athirst for an emotion, a beauty which cannot be found in its perfection upon earth, or only for a moment. His imagination, which had not been able to believe in Cuchulain's greatness, until it had brought the Great Queen, the red-eyebrowed goddess, to woo him upon the battlefield, could not be satisfied with a friendship less romantic and lyrical than that of Cuchulain and Ferdiad, who kissed one another after the day's fighting, or with a love less romantic and lyrical than that of Baile and Aillinn, who died at the report of one another's deaths, and married in Tir-nan-og. His art, too, is often at its greatest when it is most extravagant, for he only feels himself among solid things, among things with fixed laws and satisfying purposes, when he has reshaped the world according to his heart's desire. He understands as well as Blake that the ruins of time build mansions in eternity, and he never allows anything, that we can see and handle, to remain long unchanged. The characters must remain the same, but the strength of Fergus may change so greatly, that he, who a moment before was merely a strong man among many, becomes the master of Three Blows that would destroy an army, did they not cut off the heads of three little hills instead, and his sword, which a fool had been able to steal out of its sheath, has of a sudden the likeness of a rainbow. A wandering lyric moon must knead and kindle perpetually that moving world of cloaks made out of the fleeces of Mananan; of armed men who change themselves into sea-birds; of goddesses who become crows; of trees that bear fruit and flower at the same time. The great emotions of love, terror and friendship must alone remain untroubled by the moon in that world which is still the world of the Irish country-people, who do not open their eyes very wide at the most miraculous change, at the most sudden enchantment. Its events, and things, and people are wild, and are like unbroken horses, that are so much more beautiful than horses that have learned to run between shafts. One thinks of actual life, when one reads those Norse stories, which had shadows of their decadence, so necessary were the proportions of actual life to their efforts, when a dying man remembered his heroism enough to look down at his wound and say, 'Those broad spears are coming into fashion'; but the Irish stories make us understand why some Greek writer called myths the activities of the dæmons. The great virtues, the great joys, the great privations, come in the myths, and, as it were, take mankind between their naked arms, and without putting off their divinity. Poets have chosen their themes more often from stories that are all, or half, mythological, than from history or stories that give one the sensation of history, understanding, as I think, that the imagination which remembers the proportions of life is but a long wooing, and that it has to forget them before it becomes the torch and the marriage-bed.

One finds, as one expects, in the work of men who were not troubled about any probabilities or necessities but those of emotion itself, an immense variety of incident and character and of ways of expressing emotion. Cuchulain fights man after man during the quest of the Brown Bull, and not one of those fights is like another, and not one is lacking in emotion or strangeness; and when one thinks imagination can do no more, the story of the Two Bulls, emblematic of all contests, suddenly lifts romance into prophecy. The characters too have a distinctness we do not find among the people of the Mabinogion, perhaps not even among the people of the Morte D'Arthur. We know we shall be long forgetting Cuchulain, whose life is vehement and full of pleasure, as though he always remembered that it was to be soon over; or the dreamy Fergus who betrays the sons of Usnach for a feast, without ceasing to be noble; or Conal who is fierce and friendly and trustworthy, but has not the sap of divinity that makes Cuchulain mysterious to men, and beloved of women. Women indeed, with their lamentations for lovers and husbands and sons, and for fallen rooftrees and lost wealth, give the stories their most beautiful sentences; and, after Cuchulain, one thinks most of certain great queens,of angry, amorous Mæve, with her long, pale face; of Findabair, her daughter, who dies of shame and of pity; of Deirdre, who might be some mild modern housewife but for her prophetic wisdom. If one does not set Deirdre's lamentations among the greatest lyric poems of the world, I think one may be certain that the wine-press of the poets has been trodden for one in vain; and yet I think it may be proud Emer, Cuchulain's fitting wife, who will linger longest in the memory. What a pure flame burns in her always, whether she is the newly-married wife fighting for precedence, fierce as some beautiful bird, or the confident housewife, who would awaken her husband from his magic sleep with mocking words; or the great queen who would get him out of the tightening net of his doom, by sending him into the Valley of the Deaf, with Niamh, his mistress, because he will be more obedient to her; or the woman whom sorrow has set with Helen and Iseult and Brunnhilda, and Deirdre, to share their immortality in the rosary of the poets.

"And oh! my love!" she said, "we were often in one another's company, and it was happy for us; for if the world had been searched from the rising of the sun to sunset, the like would never have been found in one place, of the Black Sainglain and the Grey of Macha, and Laeg the chariot-driver, and myself and Cuchulain."

'And after that Emer bade Conal to make a wide, very deep grave for Cuchulain; and she laid herself down beside her gentle comrade, and she put her mouth to his mouth, and she said: "Love of my life, my friend, my sweetheart, my one choice of the men of the earth, many is the woman, wed or unwed, envied me until to-day; and now I will not stay living after you."'

To us Irish, these personages should be very moving, very important, for they lived in the places where we ride and go marketing, and sometimes they have met one another on the hills that cast their shadows upon our doors at evening. If we will but tell these stories to our children the Land will begin again to be a Holy Land, as it was before men gave their hearts to Greece and Rome and Judea. When I was a child I had only to climb the hill behind the house to see long, blue, ragged hills flowing along the southern horizon. What beauty was lost to me, what depth of emotion is still perhaps lacking in me, because nobody told me, not even the merchant captains who knew everything, that Cruachan of the Enchantments lay behind those long, blue, ragged hills!

II

FION AND HIS CYCLE

A few months ago I was on the bare Hill of Allen, 'wide Almhuin of Leinster,' where Finn and the Fianna are said to have had their house, although there are no earthen mounds there like those that mark the sites of old houses on so many hills. A hot sun beat down upon flowering gorse and flowerless heather; and on every side except the east, where there were green trees and distant hills, one saw a level horizon and brown boglands with a few green places and here and there the glitter of water. One could imagine that had it been twilight and not early afternoon, and had there been vapours drifting and frothing where there were now but shadows of clouds, it would have set stirring in one, as few places even in Ireland can, a thought that is peculiar to Celtic romance, as I think, a thought of a mystery coming not as with Gothic nations out of the pressure of darkness, but out of great spaces and windy light. The hill of Teamhair, or Tara, as it is now called, with its green mounds and its partly-wooded sides, and its more gradual slope set among fat grazing lands, with great trees in the hedgerows, had brought before one imaginations, not of heroes who were in their youth for hundreds of years, or of women who came to them in the likeness of hunted fawns, but of kings that lived brief and politic lives, and of the five white roads that carried their armies to the lesser kingdoms of Ireland, or brought to the great fair that had given Teamhair its sovereignty all that sought justice or pleasure or had goods to barter.

It is certain that we must not confuse these kings, as did the medieval chroniclers, with those half-divine kings of Almhuin. The chroniclers, perhaps because they loved tradition too well to cast out utterly much that they dreaded as Christians, and perhaps because popular imagination had begun the mixture, have mixed one with another ingeniously, making Finn the head of a kind of Militia under Cormac MacArt, who is supposed to have reigned at Teamhair in the second century, and making Grania, who travels to enchanted houses under the cloak of Ængus, god of Love, and keeps her troubling beauty longer than did Helen hers, Cormac's daughter, and giving the stories of the Fianna, although the impossible has thrust its proud finger into them all, a curious air of precise history. It is only when we separate the stories from that medieval pedantry, that we recognise one of the oldest worlds that man has imagined, an older world certainly than we find in the stories of Cuchulain, who lived, according to the chroniclers, about the time of the birth of Christ. They are far better known, and we may be certain of the antiquity of incidents that are known in one form or another to every Gaelic-speaking countryman in Ireland or in the Highlands of Scotland. Sometimes a labourer digging near to a cromlech, or Bed of Diarmuid and Grania as it is called, will tell you a tradition that seems older and more barbaric than any description of their adventures or of themselves in written text or in story that has taken form in the mouths of professed story-tellers.

Finn and the Fianna found welcome among the court poets later than did Cuchulain; and one finds memories of Danish invasions and standing armies mixed with the imaginations of hunters and solitary fighters among great woods. We never hear of Cuchulain delighting in the hunt or in woodland things; and one imagines that the story-teller would have thought it unworthy in so great a man, who lived a well-ordered, elaborate life, and could delight in his chariot and his chariot-driver and his barley-fed horses. If he is in the woods before dawn we are not told that he cannot know the leaves of the hazel from the leaves of the oak; and when Emer laments him no wild creature comes into her thoughts but the cuckoo that cries over cultivated fields. His story must have come out of a time when the wild wood was giving way to pasture and tillage, and men had no longer a reason to consider every cry of the birds or change of the night. Finn, who was always in the woods, whose battles were but hours amid years of hunting, delighted in the 'cackling of ducks from the Lake of the Three Narrows; the scolding talk of the blackbird of Doire an Cairn; the bellowing of the ox from the Valley of the Berries; the whistle of the eagle from the Valley of Victories or from the rough branches of the Ridge of the Stream; the grouse of the heather of Cruachan; the call of the otter of Druim re Coir.' When sorrow comes upon the queens of the stories, they have sympathy for the wild birds and beasts that are like themselves: 'Credhe wife of Cael came with the others and went looking through the bodies for her comely comrade, and crying as she went. And as she was searching she saw a crane of the meadows and her two nestlings, and the cunning beast the fox watching the nestlings; and when the crane covered one of the birds to save it, he would make a rush at the other bird, the way she had to stretch herself out over the birds; and she would sooner have got her own death by the fox than the nestlings to be killed by him. And Credhe was looking at that, and she said: "It is no wonder I to have such love for my comely sweetheart, and the bird in that distress about her nestlings."'

One often hears of a horse that shivers with terror, or of a dog that howls at something a man's eyes cannot see, and men who live primitive lives where instinct does the work of reason are fully conscious of many things that we cannot perceive at all. As life becomes more orderly, more deliberate, the supernatural world sinks farther away. Although the gods come to Cuchulain, and although he is the son of one of the greatest of them, their country and his are far apart, and they come to him as god to mortal; but Finn is their equal. He is continually in their houses; he meets with Bodb Dearg, and Ængus, and Mananan, now as friend with friend, now as with an enemy he overcomes in battle; and when he has need of their help his messenger can say: 'There is not a king's son or a prince, or a leader of the Fianna of Ireland, without having a wife or a mother or a foster-mother or a sweetheart of the Tuatha de Danaan.' When the Fianna are broken up at last, after hundreds of years of hunting, it is doubtful that he dies at all, and certain that he comes again in some other shape, and Oisin, his son, is made king over a divine country. The birds and beasts that cross his path in the woods have been fighting-men or great enchanters or fair women, and in a moment can take some beautiful or terrible shape. We think of him and of his people as great-bodied men with large movements, that seem, as it were, flowing out of some deep below the shallow stream of personal impulse, men that have broad brows and quiet eyes full of confidence in a good luck that proves every day afresh that they are a portion of the strength of things. They are hardly so much individual men as portions of universal nature, like the clouds that shape themselves and reshape themselves momentarily, or like a bird between two boughs, or like the gods that have given the apples and the nuts; and yet this but brings them the nearer to us, for we can remake them in our image when we will, and the woods are the more beautiful for the thought. Do we not always fancy hunters to be something like this, and is not that why we think them poetical when we meet them of a sudden, as in these lines in Pauline?

'An old hunter   Talking with gods; or a high-crested chief   Sailing with troops of friends to Tenedos.'

One must not expect in these stories the epic lineaments, the many incidents woven into one great event of, let us say, the story of the War for the Brown Bull of Cuailgne, or that of the last gathering at Muirthemne. Even Diarmuid and Grania, which is a long story, has nothing of the clear outlines of Deirdre, and is indeed but a succession of detached episodes. The men who imagined the Fianna had the imagination of children, and as soon as they had invented one wonder, heaped another on top of it. Children or, at any rate, it is so I remember my own childhood,do not understand large design, and they delight in little shut-in places where they can play at houses more than in great expanses where a country-side takes, as it were, the impression of a thought. The wild creatures and the green things are more to them than to us, for they creep towards our light by little holes and crevices. When they imagine a country for themselves it is always a country where you can wander without aim, and where you can never know from one place what another will be like, or know from the one day's adventure what may meet you with to-morrow's sun.

Children play at being great and wonderful people, at the ambitions they will put away for one reason or another before they grow into ordinary men and women. Mankind as a whole had a like dream once; everybody and nobody built up the dream bit by bit, and the ancient story-tellers are there to make us remember what mankind would have been like, had not fear and the failing will and the laws of nature tripped up its heels. The Fianna and their like are themselves so full of power, and they are set in a world so fluctuating and dreamlike, that nothing can hold them from being all that the heart desires.

I have read in a fabulous book that Adam had but to imagine a bird and it was born into life, and that he created all things out of himself by nothing more important than an unflagging fancy; and heroes who can make a ship out of a shaving have but little less of the divine prerogatives. They have no speculative thoughts to wander through eternity and waste heroic blood; but how could that be otherwise? for it is at all times the proud angels who sit thinking upon the hill-side and not the people of Eden. One morning we meet them hunting a stag that is 'as joyful as the leaves of a tree in summertime'; and whatever they do, whether they listen to the harp or follow an enchanter over-sea, they do for the sake of joy, their joy in one another, or their joy in pride and movement; and even their battles are fought more because of their delight in a good fighter than because of any gain that is in victory. They live always as if they were playing a game; and so far as they have any deliberate purpose at all, it is that they may become great gentlemen and be worthy of the songs of the poets. It has been said, and I think the Japanese were the first to say it, that the four essential virtues are to be generous among the weak, and truthful among one's friends, and brave among one's enemies, and courteous at all times; and if we understand by courtesy not merely the gentleness the story-tellers have celebrated, but a delight in courtly things, in beautiful clothing and in beautiful verse, one understands that it was no formal succession of trials that bound the Fianna to one another. Only the Table Round, that is indeed, as it seems, a rivulet from the same well-head, is bound in a like fellowship, and there the four heroic virtues are troubled by the abstract virtues of the cloister. Every now and then some noble knight builds a cell upon the hill-side, or leaves kind women and joyful knights to seek the vision of the Grail in lonely adventures. But when Oisin or some kingly forerunner,Bran, son of Febal, or the like,rides or sails in an enchanted ship to some divine country, he but looks for a more delighted companionship, or to be in love with faces that will never fade. No thought of any life greater than that of love, and the companionship of those that have drawn their swords upon the darkness of the world, ever troubles their delight in one another as it troubles Iseult amid her love, or Arthur amid his battles. It is an ailment of our speculation that thought, when it is not the planning of something, or the doing of something, or some memory of a plain circumstance, separates us from one another because it makes us always more unlike, and because no thought passes through another's ear unchanged. Companionship can only be perfect when it is founded on things, for things are always the same under the hand, and at last one comes to hear with envy the voices of boys lighting a lantern to ensnare moths, or of the maids chattering in the kitchen about the fox that carried off a turkey before breakfast. Lady Gregory's book of tales is full of fellowship untroubled like theirs, and made noble by a courtesy that has gone perhaps out of the world. I do not know in literature better friends and lovers. When one of the Fianna finds Osgar dying the proud death of a young man, and asks is it well with him, he is answered, 'I am as you would have me be.' The very heroism of the Fianna is indeed but their pride and joy in one another, their good fellowship. Goll, old and savage, and letting himself die of hunger in a cave because he is angry and sorry, can speak lovely words to the wife whose help he refuses. 'It is best as it is,' he said, 'and I never took the advice of a woman east or west, and I never will take it. And oh, sweet-voiced queen,' he said, 'what ails you to be fretting after me? And remember now your silver and your gold, and your silks ... and do not be crying tears after me, queen with the white hands,' he said, 'but remember your constant lover Aodh, son of the best woman of the world, that came from Spain asking for you, and that I fought on Corcar-an-Dearg; and go to him now,' he said, 'for it is bad when a woman is without a good man.'

They have no asceticism, but they are more visionary than any ascetic, and their invisible life is but the life about them made more perfect and more lasting, and the invisible people are their own images in the water. Their gods may have been much besides this, for we know them from fragments of mythology picked out with trouble from a fantastic history running backward to Adam and Eve, and many things that may have seemed wicked to the monks who imagined that history, may have been altered or left out; but this they must have been essentially, for the old stories are confirmed by apparitions among the country-people to-day. The Men of Dea fought against the mis-shapen Fomor, as Finn fights against the Cat-Heads and the Dog-Heads; and when they are overcome at last by men, they make themselves houses in the hearts of hills that are like the houses of men. When they call men to their houses and to their Country Under-Wave they promise them all that they have upon earth, only in greater abundance. The god Midhir sings to Queen Etain in one of the most beautiful of the stories: 'The young never grow old; the fields and the flowers are as pleasant to be looking at as the blackbird's eggs; warm streams of mead and wine flow through that country; there is no care or no sorrow on any person; we see others, but we ourselves are not seen.' These gods are indeed more wise and beautiful than men; but men, when they are great men, are stronger than they are, for men are, as it were, the foaming tide-line of their sea. One remembers the Druid who answered, when someone asked him who made the world, 'The Druids made it.' All was indeed but one life flowing everywhere, and taking one quality here, another there. It sometimes seems as if there is a kind of day and night of religion, and that a period when the influences are those that shape the world is followed by a period when the greater power is in influences that would lure the soul out of the world, out of the body. When Oisin is speaking with St. Patrick of the friends and the life he has outlived, he can but cry out constantly against a religion that has no meaning for him. He laments, and the country-people have remembered his words for centuries: 'I will cry my fill, but not for God, but because Finn and the Fianna are not living.'

Old writers had an admirable symbolism that attributed certain energies to the influence of the sun, and certain others to the lunar influence. To lunar influence belong all thoughts and emotions that were created by the community, by the common people, by nobody knows who, and to the sun all that came from the high disciplined or individual kingly mind. I myself imagine a marriage of the sun and moon in the arts I take most pleasure in; and now bride and bridegroom but exchange, as it were, full cups of gold and silver, and now they are one in a mystical embrace. From the moon come the folk-songs imagined by reapers and spinners out of the common impulse of their labour, and made not by putting words together, but by mixing verses and phrases, and the folk-tales made by the capricious mixing of incidents known to everybody in new ways, as one deals out cards, never getting the same hand twice over. When one hears some fine story, one never knows whether it has not been hazard that put the last touch of adventure. Such poetry, as it seems to me, desires an infinity of wonder or emotion, for where there is no individual mind there is no measurer-out, no marker-in of limits. The poor fisher has no possession of the world and no responsibility for it; and if he dreams of a love-gift better than the brown shawl that seems too common for poetry, why should he not dream of a glove made from the skin of a bird, or shoes made from the skin of a herring, or a coat made from the glittering garment of the salmon? Was it not Æschylus who said he but served up fragments from the banquet of Homer? but Homer himself found the great banquet of an earthen floor and under a broken roof. We do not know who at the foundation of the world made the banquet for the first time, or who put the pack of cards into rough hands; but we do know that, unless those that have made many inventions are about to change the nature of poetry, we may have to go where Homer went if we are to sing a new song. Is it because all that is under the moon thirsts to escape out of bounds, to lose itself in some unbounded tidal stream, that the songs of the folk are mournful, and that the story of the Fianna, whenever the queens lament for their lovers, reminds us of songs that are still sung in country-places? Their grief, even when it is to be brief like Grania's, goes up into the waste places of the sky. But in supreme art, or in supreme life there is the influence of the sun too, and the sun brings with it, as old writers tell us, not merely discipline but joy; for its discipline is not of the kind the multitudes impose upon us by their weight and pressure, but the expression of the individual soul, turning itself into a pure fire and imposing its own pattern, its own music, upon the heaviness and the dumbness that is in others and in itself. When we have drunk the cold cup of the moon's intoxication, we thirst for something beyond ourselves, and the mind flows outward to a natural immensity; but if we have drunk from the hot cup of the sun, our own fulness awakens, we desire little, for wherever one goes one's heart goes too; and if any ask what music is the sweetest, we can but answer, as Finn answered, 'What happens.' And yet the songs and stories that have come from either influence are a part, neither less than the other, of the pleasure that is the bride-bed of poetry.

Gaelic-speaking Ireland, because its art has been made, not by the artist choosing his material from wherever he has a mind to, but by adding a little to something which it has taken generations to invent, has always had a popular literature. We cannot say how much that literature has done for the vigour of the race, for who can count the hands its praise of kings and high-hearted queens made hot upon the sword-hilt, or the amorous eyes it made lustful for strength and beauty? We remember indeed that when the farming people and the labourers of the towns made their last attempt to cast out England by force of arms they named themselves after the companions of Finn. Even when Gaelic has gone and the poetry with it, something of the habit of mind remains in ways of speech and thought and 'come-all-ye's' and poetical sayings; nor is it only among the poor that the old thought has been for strength or weakness. Surely these old stories, whether of Finn or Cuchulain, helped to sing the old Irish and the old Norman-Irish aristocracy to their end. They heard their hereditary poets and story-tellers, and they took to horse and died fighting against Elizabeth or against Cromwell; and when an English-speaking aristocracy had their place, it listened to no poetry indeed, but it felt about it in the popular mind an exacting and ancient tribunal, and began a play that had for spectators men and women that loved the high wasteful virtues. I do not think that their own mixed blood or the habit of their time need take all, or nearly all, credit or discredit for the impulse that made those gentlemen of the eighteenth century fight duels over pocket-handkerchiefs, and set out to play ball against the gates of Jerusalem for a wager, and scatter money before the public eye; and at last, after an epoch of such eloquence the world has hardly seen its like, lose their public spirit and their high heart, and grow querulous and selfish, as men do who have played life out not heartily but with noise and tumult. Had they known the people and the game a little better, they might have created an aristocracy in an age that has lost the understanding of the word. When one reads of the Fianna, or of Cuchulain, or of any of their like, one remembers that the fine life is always a part played finely before fine spectators. There also one notices the hot cup and the cold cup of intoxication; and when the fine spectators have ended, surely the fine players grow weary, and aristocratic life is ended. When O'Connell covered with a dark glove the hand that had killed a man in the duelling-field, he played his part; and when Alexander stayed his army marching to the conquest of the world that he might contemplate the beauty of a plane-tree, he played his part. When Osgar complained as he lay dying of the keening of the women and the old fighting-men, he too played his part; 'No man ever knew any heart in me,' he said, 'but a heart of twisted horn, and it covered with iron; but the howling of the dogs beside me,' he said, 'and the keening of the old fighting-men and the crying of the women one after another, those are the things that are vexing me.' If we would create a great community and what other game is so worth the labour? we must re-create the old foundations of life, not as they existed in that splendid misunderstanding of the eighteenth century, but as they must always exist when the finest minds and Ned the beggar and Seaghan the fool think about the same thing, although they may not think the same thought about it.

When I asked the little boy who had shown me the pathway up the Hill of Allen if he knew stories of Finn and Oisin, he said he did not, but that he had often heard his grandfather telling them to his mother in Irish. He did not know Irish, but he was learning it at school, and all the little boys he knew were learning it. In a little while he will know enough stories of Finn and Oisin to tell them to his children some day. It is the owners of the land whose children might never have known what would give them so much happiness. But now they can read Lady Gregory's book to their children, and it will make Slieve-na-man, Allen, and Benbulben, the great mountain that showed itself before me every day through all my childhood and was yet unpeopled, and half the country-sides of south and west, as populous with memories as her Cuchulain of Muirthemne will have made Dundealgan and Emain Macha and Muirthemne; and after a while somebody may even take them to some famous place and say, 'This land where your fathers lived proudly and finely should be dear and dear and again dear;' and perhaps when many names have grown musical to their ears, a more imaginative love will have taught them a better service.

III

I praise but in brief words the noble writing of these books, for words that praise a book, wherein something is done supremely well, remain, to sound in the ears of a later generation, like the foolish sound of church bells from the tower of a church when every pew is full.

1903.

PREFACE TO THE FIRST EDITION OF THE WELL OF THE SAINTS

Six years ago I was staying in a students' hotel in the Latin Quarter, and somebody, whose name I cannot recollect, introduced me to an Irishman, who, even poorer than myself, had taken a room at the top of the house. It was J. M. Synge, and I, who thought I knew the name of every Irishman who was working at literature, had never heard of him. He was a graduate of Trinity College, Dublin, too, and Trinity College does not, as a rule, produce artistic minds. He told me that he had been living in France and Germany, reading French and German Literature, and that he wished to become a writer. He had, however, nothing to show but one or two poems and impressionistic essays, full of that kind of morbidity that has its root in too much brooding over methods of expression, and ways of looking upon life, which come, not out of life, but out of literature, images reflected from mirror to mirror. He had wandered among people whose life is as picturesque as the middle ages, playing his fiddle to Italian sailors, and listening to stories in Bavarian woods, but life had cast no light into his writings. He had learned Irish years ago, but had begun to forget it, for the only language that interested him was that conventional language of modern poetry which has begun to make us all weary. I was very weary of it, for I had finished The Secret Rose, and felt how it had separated my imagination from life, sending my Red Hanrahan, who should have trodden the same roads with myself, into some undiscoverable country. I said, 'Give up Paris, you will never create anything by reading Racine, and Arthur Symons will always be a better critic of French literature. Go to the Arran Islands. Live there as if you were one of the people themselves; express a life that has never found expression.' I had just come from Arran, and my imagination was full of those grey islands where men must reap with knives because of the stones.

He went to Arran and became a part of its life, living upon salt fish and eggs, talking Irish for the most part, but listening also to the beautiful English which has grown up in Irish-speaking districts, and takes its vocabulary from the time of Malory and of the translators of the Bible, but its idiom and its vivid metaphor from Irish. When Mr. Synge began to write in this language, Lady Gregory had already used it finely in her translations of Dr. Hyde's lyrics and plays, or of old Irish literature, but she had listened with different ears. He made his own selection of word and phrase, choosing what would express his own personality. Above all, he made word and phrase dance to a very strange rhythm, which will always, till his plays have created their own tradition, be difficult to actors who have not learned it from his lips. It is essential, for it perfectly fits the drifting emotion, the dreaminess, the vague yet measureless desire, for which he would create a dramatic form. It blurs definition, clear edges, everything that comes from the will, it turns imagination from all that is of the present, like a gold background in a religious picture, and it strengthens in every emotion whatever comes to it from far off, from brooding memory and dangerous hope. When he brought The Shadow of the Glen, his first play, to the Irish National Theatre Society, the players were puzzled by the rhythm, but gradually they became certain that his woman of the glens, as melancholy as a curlew, driven to distraction by her own sensitiveness, her own fineness, could not speak with any other tongue, that all his people would change their life if the rhythm changed. Perhaps no Irish countryman had ever that exact rhythm in his voice, but certainly if Mr. Synge had been born a countryman, he would have spoken like that. It makes the people of his imagination a little disembodied; it gives them a kind of innocence even in their anger and their cursing. It is part of its maker's attitude towards the world, for while it makes the clash of wills among his persons indirect and dreamy, it helps him to see the subject-matter of his art with wise, clear-seeing, unreflecting eyes; to preserve the innocence of good art in an age of reasons and purposes. Whether he write of old beggars by the roadside, lamenting over the misery and ugliness of life, or of an old Arran woman mourning her drowned sons, or of a young wife married to an old husband, he has no wish to change anything, to reform anything; all these people pass by as before an open window, murmuring strange, exciting words.

If one has not fine construction, one has not drama, but if one has not beautiful or powerful and individual speech, one has not literature, or, at any rate, one has not great literature. Rabelais, Villon, Shakespeare, William Blake, would have known one another by their speech. Some of them knew how to construct a story, but all of them had abundant, resonant, beautiful, laughing, living speech. It is only the writers of our modern dramatic movement, our scientific dramatists, our naturalists of the stage, who have thought it possible to be like the greatest, and yet to cast aside even the poor persiflage of the comedians, and to write in the impersonal language that has come, not out of individual life, nor out of life at all, but out of necessities of commerce, of parliament, of board schools, of hurried journeys by rail.

If there are such things as decaying art and decaying institutions, their decay must begin when the element they receive into their care from the life of every man in the world, begins to rot. Literature decays when it no longer makes more beautiful, or more vivid, the language which unites it to all life, and when one finds the criticism of the student, and the purpose of the reformer, and the logic of the man of science, where there should have been the reveries of the common heart, ennobled into some raving Lear or unabashed Don Quixote. One must not forget that the death of language, the substitution of phrases as nearly impersonal as algebra for words and rhythms varying from man to man, is but a part of the tyranny of impersonal things. I have been reading through a bundle of German plays, and have found everywhere a desire not to express hopes and alarms common to every man that ever came into the world, but politics or social passion, a veiled or open propaganda. Now it is duelling that has need of reproof; now it is the ideas of an actress, returning from the free life of the stage, that must be contrasted with the prejudice of an old-fashioned town; now it is the hostility of Christianity and Paganism in our own day that is to find an obscure symbol in a bell thrown from its tower by spirits of the wood. I compare the work of these dramatists with the greater plays of their Scandinavian master, and remember that even he, who has made so many clear-drawn characters, has made us no abundant character, no man of genius in whom we could believe, and that in him also, even when it is Emperor and Galilean that are face to face, even the most momentous figures are subordinate to some tendency, to some movement, to some inanimate energy, or to some process of thought whose very logic has changed it into mechanism,always to something other than human life.

We must not measure a young talent, whether we praise or blame, with that of men who are among the greatest of our time, but we may say of any talent, following out a definition, that it takes up the tradition of great drama as it came from the hands of the masters who are acknowledged by all time, and turns away from a dramatic movement, which, though it has been served by fine talent, has been imposed upon us by science, by artificial life, by a passing order.

When the individual life no longer delights in its own energy, when the body is not made strong and beautiful by the activities of daily life, when men have no delight in decorating the body, one may be certain that one lives in a passing order, amid the inventions of a fading vitality. If Homer were alive to-day, he would only resist, after a deliberate struggle, the temptation to find his subject not in Helen's beauty, that every man has desired, nor in the wisdom and endurance of Odysseus that has been the desire of every woman that has come into the world, but in what somebody would describe, perhaps, as 'the inevitable contest,' arising out of economic causes, between the country-places and small towns on the one hand, and, upon the other, the great city of Troy, representing one knows not what 'tendency to centralisation.'

Mr. Synge has in common with the great theatre of the world, with that of Greece and that of India, with the creator of Falstaff, with Racine, a delight in language, a preoccupation with individual life. He resembles them also by a preoccupation with what is lasting and noble, that came to him, not as I think from books, but while he listened to old stories in the cottages, and contrasted what they remembered with reality. The only literature of the Irish country-people is their songs, full often of extravagant love, and their stories of kings and of kings' children. 'I will cry my fill, but not for God, but because Finn and the Fianna are not living,' says Oisin in the story. Every writer, even every small writer, who has belonged to the great tradition, has had his dream of an impossibly noble life, and the greater he is, the more does it seem to plunge him into some beautiful or bitter reverie. Some, and of these are all the earliest poets of the world, gave it direct expression; others mingle it so subtly with reality, that it is a day's work to disentangle it; others bring it near by showing one whatever is most its contrary. Mr. Synge, indeed, sets before us ugly, deformed or sinful people, but his people, moved by no practical ambition, are driven by a dream of that impossible life. That we may feel how intensely his woman of the glen dreams of days that shall be entirely alive, she that is 'a hard woman to please' must spend her days between a sour-faced old husband, a man who goes mad upon the hills, a craven lad and a drunken tramp; and those two blind people of The Well of the Saints are so transformed by the dream, that they choose blindness rather than reality. He tells us of realities, but he knows that art has never taken more than its symbols from anything that the eye can see or the hand measure.

It is the preoccupation of his characters with their dream that gives his plays their drifting movement, their emotional subtlety. In most of the dramatic writing of our time, and this is one of the reasons why our dramatists do not find the need for a better speech, one finds a simple motive lifted, as it were, into the full light of the stage. The ordinary student of drama will not find anywhere in The Well of the Saints that excitement of the will in the presence of attainable advantages, which he is accustomed to think the natural stuff of drama, and if he see it played he will wonder why act is knitted to act so loosely, why it is all, as it were, flat, why there is so much leisure in the dialogue, even in the midst of passion. If he see the Shadow of the Glen, he will ask, why does this woman go out of her house? Is it because she cannot help herself, or is she content to go? Why is it not all made clearer? And yet, like everybody when caught up into great events, she does many things without being quite certain why she does them. She hardly understands at moments why her action has a certain form, more clearly than why her body is tall or short, fair or brown. She feels an emotion that she does not understand. She is driven by desires that need for their expression, not 'I admire this man,' or 'I must go, whether I will or no,' but words full of suggestion, rhythms of voice, movements that escape analysis. In addition to all this, she has something that she shares with none but the children of one man's imagination. She is intoxicated by a dream which is hardly understood by herself, but possesses her like something half remembered on a sudden wakening.

While I write, we are rehearsing The Well of the Saints, and are painting for it decorative scenery, mountains in one or two flat colours and without detail, ash trees and red salleys with something of recurring pattern in their woven boughs. For though the people of the play use no phrase they could not use in daily life, we know that we are seeking to express what no eye has ever seen.

ABBEY THEATRE, January 27, 1905.

DISCOVERIES

PROPHET, PRIEST AND KING

The little theatrical company I write my plays for had come to a west of Ireland town, and was to give a performance in an old ball-room, for there was no other room big enough. I went there from a neighbouring country-house, and, arriving a little before the players, tried to open a window. My hands were black with dirt in a moment, and presently a pane of glass and a part of the window-frame came out in my hands. Everything in this room was half in ruins, the rotten boards cracked under my feet, and our new proscenium and the new boards of the platform looked out of place, and yet the room was not really old, in spite of the musicians' gallery over the stage. It had been built by some romantic or philanthropic landlord some three or four generations ago, and was a memory of we knew not what unfinished scheme.

From there I went to look for the players, and called for information on a young priest, who had invited them and taken upon himself the finding of an audience. He lived in a high house with other priests, and as I went in I noticed with a whimsical pleasure a broken pane of glass in the fanlight over the door, for he had once told me the story of an old woman who a good many years ago quarrelled with the bishop, got drunk and hurled a stone through the painted glass. He was a clever man who read Meredith and Ibsen, but some of his books had been packed in the fire-grate by his housekeeper, instead of the customary view of an Italian lake or the coloured tissue-paper. The players, who had been giving a performance in a neighbouring town, had not yet come, or were unpacking their costumes and properties at the hotel he had recommended them. We should have time, he said, to go through the half-ruined town and to visit the convent schools and the cathedral, where, owing to his influence, two of our young Irish sculptors had been set to carve an altar and the heads of pillars. I had only heard of this work, and I found its strangeness and simplicity,one of them had been Rodin's pupil,could not make me forget the meretriciousness of the architecture and the commercial commonplace of the inlaid pavement. The new movement had seized on the cathedral midway in its growth, and the worst of the old and the best of the new were side by side without any sign of transition. The convent school was, as other like places have been to me, a long room in a workhouse hospital at Portumna, in particular, a delight to the imagination and the eyes. A new floor had been put into some ecclesiastical building and the light from a great mullioned window, cut off at the middle, fell aslant upon rows of clean and seemingly happy children. The nuns, who show in their own convents, where they can put what they like, a love of what is mean and pretty, make beautiful rooms where the regulations compel them to do all with a few colours and a few flowers. I think it was that day, but am not sure, that I had lunch at a convent and told fairy stories to a couple of nuns, and I hope it was not mere politeness that made them seem to have a child's interest in such things.

A good many of our audience, when the curtain went up in the old ball-room, were drunk, but all were attentive, for they had a great deal of respect for my friend, and there were other priests there. Presently the man at the door opposite to the stage strayed off somewhere and I took his place, and when boys came up offering two or three pence and asking to be let into the sixpenny seats, I let them join the melancholy crowd. The play professed to tell of the heroic life of ancient Ireland, but was really full of sedentary refinement and the spirituality of cities. Every emotion was made as dainty-footed and dainty-fingered as might be, and a love and pathos where passion had faded into sentiment, emotions of pensive and harmless people, drove shadowy young men through the shadows of death and battle. I watched it with growing rage. It was not my own work, but I have sometimes watched my own work with a rage made all the more salt in the mouth from being half despair. Why should we make so much noise about ourselves and yet have nothing to say that was not better said in that workhouse dormitory, where a few flowers and a few coloured counterpanes and the coloured walls had made a severe and gracious beauty? Presently the play was changed and our comedian began to act a little farce, and when I saw him struggle to wake into laughter an audience out of whom the life had run as if it were water, I rejoiced, as I had over that broken window-pane. Here was something secular, abounding, even a little vulgar, for he was gagging horribly, condescending to his audience, though not without contempt.

We had supper in the priest's house, and a government official who had come down from Dublin, partly out of interest in this attempt 'to educate the people,' and partly because it was his holiday and it was necessary to go somewhere, entertained us with little jokes. Somebody, not, I think, a priest, talked of the spiritual destiny of our race and praised the night's work, for the play was refined and the people really very attentive, and he could not understand my discontent; but presently he was silenced by the patter of jokes.

I had my breakfast by myself the next morning, for the players had got up in the middle of the night and driven some ten miles to catch an early train to Dublin, and were already on their way to their shops and offices. I had brought the visitors' book of the hotel, to turn over its pages while waiting for my bacon and eggs, and found several pages full of obscenities, scrawled there some two or three weeks before, by Dublin visitors, it seemed, for a notorious Dublin street was mentioned. Nobody had thought it worth his while to tear out the page or blacken out the lines, and as I put the book away impressions that had been drifting through my mind for months rushed up into a single thought. 'If we poets are to move the people, we must reintegrate the human spirit in our imagination. The English have driven away the kings, and turned the prophets into demagogues, and you cannot have health among a people if you have not prophet, priest and king.'

My work in Ireland has continually set this thought before me: 'How can I make my work mean something to vigorous and simple men whose attention is not given to art but to a shop, or teaching in a National School, or dispensing medicine?' I had not wanted to 'elevate them' or 'educate them,' as these words are understood, but to make them understand my vision, and I had not wanted a large audience, certainly not what is called a national audience, but enough people for what is accidental and temporary to lose itself in the lump. In England, where there have been so many changing activities and so much systematic education, one only escapes from crudities and temporary interests among students, but here there is the right audience, could one but get its ears. I have always come to this certainty: what moves natural men in the arts is what moves them in life, and that is, intensity of personal life, intonations that show them in a book or a play, the strength, the essential moment of a man who would be exciting in the market or at the dispensary door. They must go out of the theatre with the strength they live by strengthened with looking upon some passion that could, whatever its chosen way of life, strike down an enemy, fill a long stocking with money or move a girl's heart. They have not much to do with the speculations of science, though they have a little, or with the speculations of metaphysics, though they have a little. Their legs will tire on the road if there is nothing in their hearts but vague sentiment, and though it is charming to have an affectionate feeling about flowers, that will not pull the cart out of the ditch. An exciting person, whether the hero of a play or the maker of poems, will display the greatest volume of personal energy, and this energy must seem to come out of the body as out of the mind. We must say to ourselves continually when we imagine a character: 'Have I given him the roots, as it were, of all faculties necessary for life?' And only when one is certain of that may one give him the one faculty that fills the imagination with joy. I even doubt if any play had ever a great popularity that did not use, or seem to use, the bodily energies of its principal actor to the full. Villon the robber could have delighted these Irishmen with plays and songs, if he and they had been born to the same traditions of word and symbol, but Shelley could not; and as men came to live in towns and to read printed books and to have many specialised activities, it has become more possible to produce Shelleys and less and less possible to produce Villons. The last Villon dwindled into Robert Burns because the highest faculties had faded, taking the sense of beauty with them, into some sort of vague heaven and left the lower to lumber where they best could. In literature, partly from the lack of that spoken word which knits us to normal man, we have lost in personality, in our delight in the whole man, blood, imagination, intellect, running together, but have found a new delight, in essences, in states of mind, in pure imagination, in all that comes to us most easily in elaborate music. There are two ways before literature, upward into ever-growing subtlety, with Verhaeren, with Mallarmé, with Maeterlinck, until at last, it may be, a new agreement among refined and studious men gives birth to a new passion, and what seems literature becomes religion; or downward, taking the soul with us until all is simplified and solidified again. That is the choice of choices, the way of the bird until common eyes have lost us, or to the market carts; but we must see to it that the soul goes with us, for the bird's song is beautiful, and the traditions of modern imagination, growing always more musical, more lyrical, more melancholy, casting up now a Shelley, now a Swinburne, now a Wagner, are, it may be, the frenzy of those that are about to see what the magic hymn printed by the Abbé de Villars has called the Crown of Living and Melodious Diamonds. If the carts have hit our fancy we must have the soul tight within our bodies, for it has grown so fond of a beauty accumulated by subtle generations that it will for a long time be impatient with our thirst for mere force, mere personality, for the tumult of the blood. If it begin to slip away we must go after it, for Shelley's Chapel of the Morning Star is better than Burns's beer-house, surely it was beer, not barleycorn, except at the day's weary end; and it is always better than that uncomfortable place where there is no beer, the machine shop of the realists.

THE MUSICIAN AND THE ORATOR

Walter Pater says music is the type of all the Arts, but somebody else, I forget now who, that oratory is their type. You will side with the one or the other according to the nature of your energy, and I in my present mood am all for the man who, with an average audience before him, uses all means of persuasion,stories, laughter, tears, and but so much music as he can discover on the wings of words. I would even avoid the conversation of the lovers of music, who would draw us into the impersonal land of sound and colour, and I would have no one write with a sonata in his memory. We may even speak a little evil of musicians, having admitted that they will see before we do that melodious crown. We may remind them that the housemaid does not respect the piano-tuner as she does the plumber, and of the enmity that they have aroused among all poets. Music is the most impersonal of things, and words the most personal, and that is why musicians do not like words. They masticate them for a long time, being afraid they would not be able to digest them, and when the words are so broken and softened and mixed with spittle that they are not words any longer, they swallow them.

A GUITAR PLAYER

A girl has been playing on the guitar. She is pretty, and if I didn't listen to her I could have watched her, and if I didn't watch her I could have listened. Her voice, the movements of her body, the expression of her face, all said the same thing. A player of a different temper and body would have made all different, and might have been delightful in some other way. A movement not of music only but of life came to its perfection. I was delighted and I did not know why until I thought, 'That is the way my people, the people I see in the mind's eye, play music, and I like it because it is all personal, as personal as Villon's poetry.' The little instrument is quite light, and the player can move freely and express a joy that is not of the fingers and the mind only but of the whole being; and all the while her movements call up into the mind, so erect and natural she is, whatever is most beautiful in her daily life. Nearly all the old instruments were like that, even the organ was once a little instrument, and when it grew big our wise forefathers gave it to God in the cathedrals, where it befits Him to be everything. But if you sit at the piano, it is the piano, the mechanism, that is the important thing, and nothing of you means anything but your fingers and your intellect.

THE LOOKING-GLASS

I have just been talking to a girl with a shrill monotonous voice and an abrupt way of moving. She is fresh from school, where they have taught her history and geography 'whereby a soul can be discerned,' but what is the value of an education, or even in the long run of a science, that does not begin with the personality, the habitual self, and illustrate all by that? Somebody should have taught her to speak for the most part on whatever note of her voice is most musical, and soften those harsh notes by speaking, not singing, to some stringed instrument, taking note after note and, as it were, caressing her words a little as if she loved the sound of them, and have taught her after this some beautiful pantomimic dance, till it had grown a habit to live for eye and ear. A wise theatre might make a training in strong and beautiful life the fashion, teaching before all else the heroic discipline of the looking-glass, for is not beauty, even as lasting love, one of the most difficult of the arts?

THE TREE OF LIFE

We artists have taken over-much to heart that old commandment about seeking after the Kingdom of Heaven. Verlaine told me that he had tried to translate 'In Memoriam,' but could not because Tennyson was 'too noble, too Anglais, and, when he should have been broken-hearted, had many reminiscences.' About that time I found in some English review an essay of his on Shakespeare. 'I had once a fine Shakespeare,' he wrote, or some such words, 'but I have it no longer. I write from memory.' One wondered in what vicissitude he had sold it, and for what money; and an image of the man rose in the imagination. To be his ordinary self as much as possible, not a scholar or even a reader, that was certainly his pose; and in the lecture he gave at Oxford he insisted 'that the poet should hide nothing of himself,' though he must speak it all with 'a care of that dignity which should manifest itself, if not in the perfection of form, at all events with an invisible, insensible, but effectual endeavour after this lofty and severe quality, I was about to say this virtue.' It was this feeling for his own personality, his delight in singing his own life, even more than that life itself, which made the generation I belong to compare him to Villon. It was not till after his death that I understood the meaning his words should have had for me, for while he lived I was interested in nothing but states of mind, lyrical moments, intellectual essences. I would not then have been as delighted as I am now by that guitar player, or as shocked as I am now by that girl whose movements have grown abrupt, and whose voice has grown harsh by the neglect of all but external activities. I had not learned what sweetness, what rhythmic movement, there is in those who have become the joy that is themselves. Without knowing it, I had come to care for nothing but impersonal beauty. I had set out on life with the thought of putting my very self into poetry, and had understood this as a representation of my own visions and an attempt to cut away the non-essential, but as I imagined the visions outside myself my imagination became full of decorative landscape and of still life. I thought of myself as something unmoving and silent living in the middle of my own mind and body, a grain of sand in Bloomsbury or in Connacht that Satan's watch fiends cannot find. Then one day I understood quite suddenly, as the way is, that I was seeking something unchanging and unmixed and always outside myself, a Stone or an Elixir that was always out of reach, and that I myself was the fleeting thing that held out its hand. The more I tried to make my art deliberately beautiful, the more did I follow the opposite of myself, for deliberate beauty is like a woman always desiring man's desire. Presently I found that I entered into myself and pictured myself and not some essence when I was not seeking beauty at all, but merely to lighten the mind of some burden of love or bitterness thrown upon it by the events of life. We are only permitted to desire life, and all the rest should be our complaints or our praise of that exacting mistress who can awake our lips into song with her kisses. But we must not give her all, we must deceive her a little at times, for, as Le Sage says in Diable Boiteux the false lovers who do not become melancholy or jealous with honest passion have the happiest mistresses and are rewarded the soonest and by the most beautiful. Our deceit will give us style, mastery, that dignity, that lofty and severe quality Verlaine spoke of. To put it otherwise, we should ascend out of common interests, the thoughts of the newspapers, of the marketplace, of men of science, but only so far as we can carry the normal, passionate, reasoning self, the personality as a whole. We must find some place upon the Tree of Life for the Phoenix nest, for the passion that is exaltation and the negation of the will, for the wings that are always upon fire, set high that the forked branches may keep it safe, yet low enough to be out of the little wind-tossed boughs, the quivering of the twigs.

THE PRAISE OF OLD WIVES' TALES

An art may become impersonal because it has too much circumstance or too little, because the world is too little or too much with it, because it is too near the ground or too far up among the branches. I met an old man out fishing a year ago, who said to me, 'Don Quixote and Odysseus are always near to me'; that is true for me also, for even Hamlet and Lear and Oedipus are more cloudy.[1] No playwright ever has made or ever will make a character that will follow us out of the theatre as Don Quixote follows us out of the book, for no playwright can be wholly episodical, and when one constructs, bringing one's characters into complicated relations with one another, something impersonal comes into the story. Society, fate, 'tendency,' something not quite human, begins to arrange the characters and to excite into action only so much of their humanity as they find it necessary to show to one another. The common heart will always love better the tales that have something of an old wives' tale and that look upon their hero from every side as if he alone were wonderful, as a child does with a new penny. In plays of a comedy too extravagant to photograph life, or written in verse, the construction is of a necessity woven out of naked motives and passions, but when an atmosphere of modern reality has to be built up as well, and the tendency, or fate, or society has to be shown as it is about ourselves, the characters grow fainter, and we have to read the book many times or see the play many times before we can remember them. Even then they are only possible in a certain drawing-room and among such and such people, and we must carry all that lumber in our heads. I thought Tolstoi's 'War and Peace' the greatest story I had ever read, and yet it has gone from me; even Lancelot, ever a shadow, is more visible in my memory than all its substance.

THE PLAY OF MODERN MANNERS

Of all artistic forms that have had a large share of the world's attention, the worst is the play about modern educated people. Except where it is superficial or deliberately argumentative it fills one's soul with a sense of commonness as with dust. It has one mortal ailment. It cannot become impassioned, that is to say, vital, without making somebody gushing and sentimental. Educated and well-bred people do not wear their hearts upon their sleeves, and they have no artistic and charming language except light persiflage and no powerful language at all, and when they are deeply moved they look silently into the fireplace. Again and again I have watched some play of this sort with growing curiosity through the opening scene. The minor people argue, chaff one another, hint sometimes at some deeper stream of life just as we do in our houses, and I am content. But all the time I have been wondering why the chief character, the man who is to bear the burden of fate, is gushing, sentimental and quite without ideas. Then the great scene comes and I understand that he cannot be well-bred or self-possessed or intellectual, for if he were he would draw a chair to the fire and there would be no duologue at the end of the third act. Ibsen understood the difficulty and made all his characters a little provincial that they might not put each other out of countenance, and made a leading article sort of poetry, phrases about vine leaves and harps in the air it was possible to believe them using in their moments of excitement, and if the play needed more than that, they could always do something stupid. They could go out and hoist a flag as they do at the end of Little Eyolf. One only understands that this manner, deliberately adopted one doubts not, had gone into his soul and filled it with dust, when one has noticed that he could no longer create a man of genius. The happiest writers are those that, knowing this form of play to be slight and passing, keep to the surface, never showing anything but the arguments and the persiflage of daily observation, or now and then, instead of the expression of passion, a stage picture, a man holding a woman's hand or sitting with his head in his hands in dim light by the red glow of a fire. It was certainly an understanding of the slightness of the form, of its incapacity for the expression of the deeper sorts of passion, that made the French invent the play with a thesis, for where there is a thesis people can grow hot in argument, almost the only kind of passion that displays itself in our daily life. The novel of contemporary educated life is upon the other hand a permanent form because having the power of psychological description it can follow the thought of a man who is looking into the grate.

HAS THE DRAMA OF CONTEMPORARY LIFE A ROOT OF ITS OWN?

In watching a play about modern educated people, with its meagre language and its action crushed into the narrow limits of possibility, I have found myself constantly saying: 'Maybe it has its power to move, slight as that is, from being able to suggest fundamental contrasts and passions which romantic and poetical literature have shown to be beautiful.' A man facing his enemies alone in a quarrel over the purity of the water in a Norwegian Spa and using no language but that of the newspapers can call up into our minds, let us say, the passion of Coriolanus. The lovers and fighters of old imaginative literature are more vivid experiences in the soul than anything but one's own ruling passion that is itself riddled by their thought as by lightning, and even two dumb figures on the roads can call up all that glory. Put the man who has no knowledge of literature before a play of this kind and he will say, as he has said in some form or other in every age at the first shock of naturalism, 'What has brought me out to hear nothing but the words we use at home when we are talking of the rates?' And he will prefer to it any play where there is visible beauty or mirth, where life is exciting, at high tide as it were. It is not his fault that he will prefer in all likelihood a worse play although its kind may be greater, for we have been following the lure of science for generations and forgotten him and his. I come always back to this thought. There is something of an old wives' tale in fine literature. The makers of it are like an old peasant telling stories of the great famine or the hangings of '98 or his own memories. He has felt something in the depth of his mind and he wants to make it as visible and powerful to our senses as possible. He will use the most extravagant words or illustrations if they suit his purpose. Or he will invent a wild parable, and the more his mind is on fire or the more creative it is, the less will he look at the outer world or value it for its own sake. It gives him metaphors and examples, and that is all. He is even a little scornful of it, for it seems to him while the fit is on that the fire has gone out of it and left it but white ashes. I cannot explain it, but I am certain that every high thing was invented in this way, between sleeping and waking, as it were, and that peering and peeping persons are but hawkers of stolen goods. How else could their noses have grown so ravenous or their eyes so sharp?

WHY THE BLIND MAN IN ANCIENT TIMES WAS MADE A POET

A description in the Iliad or the Odyssey, unlike one in the Æneid or in most modern writers, is the swift and natural observation of a man as he is shaped by life. It is a refinement of the primary hungers and has the least possible of what is merely scholarly or exceptional. It is, above all, never too observant, too professional, and when the book is closed we have had our energies enriched, for we have been in the mid-current. We have never seen anything Odysseus could not have seen while his thought was of the Cyclops, or Achilles when Briseis moved him to desire. In the art of the greatest periods there is something careless and sudden in all habitual moods though not in their expression, because these moods are a conflagration of all the energies of active life. In primitive times the blind man became a poet as he became a fiddler in our villages, because he had to be driven out of activities all his nature cried for before he could be contented with the praise of life. And often it is Villon or Verlaine with impediments plain to all, who sings of life with the ancient simplicity. Poets of coming days, when once more it will be possible to write as in the great epochs, will recognise that their sacrifice shall be to refuse what blindness and evil name, or imprisonment at the outsetting, denied to men who missed thereby the sting of a deliberate refusal. The poets of the ages of silver need no refusal of life, the dome of many-coloured glass is already shattered while they live. They look at life deliberately and as if from beyond life, and the greatest of them need suffer nothing but the sadness that the saints have known. This is their aim, and their temptation is not a passionate activity, but the approval of their fellows, which comes to them in full abundance only when they delight in the general thoughts that hold together a cultivated middle-class, where irresponsibilities of position and poverty are lacking; the things that are more excellent among educated men who have political preoccupations, Augustus Cæsar's affability, all that impersonal fecundity which muddies the intellectual passions. Ben Jonson says in the 'Poetaster,' that even the best of men without Promethean fire is but a hollow statue, and a studious man will commonly forget after some forty winters that of a certainty Promethean fire will burn somebody's fingers. It may happen that poets will be made more often by their sins than by their virtues, for general praise is unlucky, as the villages know, and not merely as I imagine, for I am superstitious about these things, because the praise of all but an equal enslaves and adds a pound to the ball at the ankle with every compliment.

All energy that comes from the whole man is as irregular as the lightning, for the communicable and forecastable and discoverable is a part only, a hungry chicken under the breast of the pelican, and the test of poetry is not in reason but in a delight not different from the delight that comes to a man at the first coming of love into the heart. I knew an old man who had spent his whole life cutting hazel and privet from the paths, and in some seventy years he had observed little but had many imaginations. He had never seen like a naturalist, never seen things as they are, for his habitual mood had been that of a man stirred in his affairs; and Shakespeare, Tintoretto, though the times were running out when Tintoretto painted, nearly all the great men of the Renaissance, looked at the world with eyes like his. Their minds were never quiescent, never as it were in a mood for scientific observations, always an exaltation, never, to use known words, founded upon an elimination of the personal factor; and their attention and the attention of those they worked for dwelt constantly with what is present to the mind in exaltation. I am too modern fully to enjoy Tintoretto's 'Creation of the Milky Way,' I cannot fix my thoughts upon that glowing and palpitating flesh intently enough to forget, as I can the make-believe of a fairy tale, that heavy drapery hanging from a cloud, though I find my pleasure in King Lear heightened by the make-believe that comes upon it all when the fool says: 'This prophecy Merlin shall make, for I live before his time'; and I always find it quite natural, so little does logic in the mere circumstance matter in the finest art, that Richard's and Richmond's tents should be side by side. I saw with delight The Knight of the Burning Pestle when Mr. Carr revived it, and found it none the worse because the apprentice acted a whole play upon the spur of the moment and without committing a line to heart. When Ben Jonson's Epicoene rammed a century of laughter into the two hours' traffic, I found with amazement that almost every journalist had put logic on the seat, where our lady imagination should pronounce that unjust and favouring sentence her woman's heart is ever plotting, and had felt bound to cherish none but reasonable sympathies and to resent the baiting of that grotesque old man. I have been looking over a book of engravings made in the eighteenth century from those wall-pictures of Herculaneum and Pompeii that were, it seems, the work of journeymen copying from finer paintings, for the composition is always too good for the execution. I find in great numbers an indifference to obvious logic, to all that the eye sees at common moments. Perseus shows Andromeda the death she lived by in a pool, and though the lovers are carefully drawn the reflection is upside down that we may see it the better. There is hardly an old master who has not made known to us in some like way how little he cares for what every fool can see and every knave can praise. The men who imagined the arts were not less superstitious in religion, understanding the spiritual relations, but not the mechanical, and finding nothing that need strain the throat in those gnats the floods of Noah and Deucalion, and in Joshua's moon at Ascalon.

CONCERNING SAINTS AND ARTISTS

I took the Indian hemp with certain followers of St. Martin on the ground floor of a house in the Latin Quarter. I had never taken it before, and was instructed by a boisterous young poet, whose English was no better than my French. He gave me a little pellet, if I am not forgetting, an hour before dinner, and another after we had dined together at some restaurant. As we were going through the streets to the meeting-place of the Martinists, I felt suddenly that a cloud I was looking at floated in an immense space, and for an instant my being rushed out, as it seemed, into that space with ecstasy. I was myself again immediately, but the poet was wholly above himself, and presently he pointed to one of the street lamps now brightening in the fading twilight, and cried at the top of his voice, 'Why do you look at me with your great eye?' There were perhaps a dozen people already much excited when we arrived; and after I had drunk some cups of coffee and eaten a pellet or two more, I grew very anxious to dance, but did not, as I could not remember any steps. I sat down and closed my eyes; but no, I had no visions, nothing but a sensation of some dark shadow which seemed to be telling me that someday I would go into a trance and so out of my body for a while, but not yet. I opened my eyes and looked at some red ornament on the mantelpiece, and at once the room was full of harmonies of red, but when a blue china figure caught my eye the harmonies became blue upon the instant. I was puzzled, for the reds were all there, nothing had changed, but they were no longer important or harmonious; and why had the blues so unimportant but a moment ago become exciting and delightful? Thereupon it struck me that I was seeing like a painter, and that in the course of the evening everyone there would change through every kind of artistic perception.

After a while a Martinist ran towards me with a piece of paper on which he had drawn a circle with a dot in it, and pointing at it with his finger he cried out, 'God, God!' Some immeasurable mystery had been revealed, and his eyes shone; and at some time or other a lean and shabby man, with rather a distinguished face, showed me his horoscope and pointed with an ecstasy of melancholy at its evil aspects. The boisterous poet, who was an old eater of the Indian hemp, had told me that it took one three months growing used to it, three months more enjoying it, and three months being cured of it. These men were in their second period; but I never forgot myself, never really rose above myself for more than a moment, and was even able to feel the absurdity of that gaiety, an Herr Nordau among the men of genius, but one that was abashed at his own sobriety. The sky outside was beginning to grey when there came a knocking at the window shutters. Somebody opened the window, and a woman in evening dress, who was not a little bewildered to find so many people, was helped down into the room. She had been at a students' ball unknown to her husband, who was asleep overhead, and had thought to have crept home unobserved, but for a confederate at the window. All those talking or dancing men laughed in a dreamy way; and she, understanding that there was no judgment in the laughter of men that had no thought but of the spectacle of the world, blushed, laughed and darted through the room and so upstairs. Alas that the hangman's rope should be own brother to that Indian happiness that keeps alone, were it not for some stray cactus, mother of as many dreams, immemorial impartiality.

THE SUBJECT MATTER OF DRAMA

I read this sentence a few days ago, or one like it, in an obituary of Ibsen: 'Let nobody again go back to the old ballad material of Shakespeare, to murders, and ghosts, for what interests us on the stage is modern experience and the discussion of our interests;' and in another part of the article Ibsen was blamed because he had written of suicides and in other ways made use of 'the morbid terror of death.' Dramatic literature has for a long time been left to the criticism of journalists, and all these, the old stupid ones and the new clever ones, have tried to impress upon it their absorption in the life of the moment, their delight in obvious originality and in obvious logic, their shrinking from the ancient and insoluble. The writer I have quoted is much more than a journalist, but he has lived their hurried life, and instinctively turns to them for judgment. He is not thinking of the great poets and painters, of the cloud of witnesses, who are there that we may become, through our understanding of their minds, spectators of the ages, but of this age. Drama is a means of expression, not a special subject matter, and the dramatist is as free to choose where he has a mind to, as the poet of 'Endymion,' or as the painter of Mary Magdalene at the door of Simon the Pharisee. So far from the discussion of our interests and the immediate circumstance of our life being the most moving to the imagination, it is what is old and far off that stirs us the most deeply. There is a sentence in The Marriage of Heaven and Hell that is meaningless until we understand Blake's system of correspondences. 'The best wine is the oldest, the best water the newest.'

Water is experience, immediate sensation, and wine is emotion, and it is with the intellect, as distinguished from imagination, that we enlarge the bounds of experience and separate it from all but itself, from illusion, from memory, and create among other things science and good journalism. Emotion, on the other hand, grows intoxicating and delightful after it has been enriched with the memory of old emotions, with all the uncounted flavours of old experience; and it is necessarily some antiquity of thought, emotions that have been deepened by the experiences of many men of genius, that distinguishes the cultivated man. The subject matter of his meditation and invention is old, and he will disdain a too conscious originality in the arts as in those matters of daily life where, is it not Balzac who says, 'we are all conservatives'? He is above all things well-bred, and whether he write or paint will not desire a technique that denies or obtrudes his long and noble descent. Corneille and Racine did not deny their masters, and when Dante spoke of his master Virgil there was no crowing of the cock. In their day imitation was conscious or all but conscious, and while originality was but so much the more a part of the man himself, so much the deeper because unconscious, no quick analysis could find out their miracle, that needed, it may be, generations to reveal; but it is our imitation that is unconscious and that waits the certainties of time. The more religious the subject matter of an art, the more will it be as it were stationary, and the more ancient will be the emotion that it arouses and the circumstances that it calls up before our eyes. When in the Middle Ages the pilgrim to St. Patrick's Purgatory found himself on the lake side, he found a boat made out of a hollow tree to ferry him to the cave of vision. In religious painting and poetry, crowns and swords of an ancient pattern take upon themselves new meanings, and it is impossible to separate our idea of what is noble from a mystic stair, where not men and women, but robes, jewels, incidents, ancient utilities float upward slowly over the all but sleeping mind, putting on emotional and spiritual life as they ascend until they are swallowed up by some far glory that they even were too modern and momentary to endure. All art is dream, and what the day is done with is dreaming ripe, and what art has moulded religion accepts, and in the end all is in the wine cup, all is in the drunken phantasy, and the grapes begin to stammer.

THE TWO KINDS OF ASCETICISM

It is not possible to separate an emotion or a spiritual state from the image that calls it up and gives it expression. Michael Angelo's Moses, Velasquez' Philip the Second, the colour purple, a crucifix, call into life an emotion or state that vanishes with them because they are its only possible expression, and that is why no mind is more valuable than the images it contains. The imaginative writer differs from the saint in that he identifies himself, to the neglect of his own soul, alas! with the soul of the world, and frees himself from all that is impermanent in that soul, an ascetic not of women and wine, but of the newspapers. That which is permanent in the soul of the world upon the other hand, the great passions that trouble all and have but a brief recurring life of flower and seed in any man, is the renunciation of the saint who seeks not an eternal art, but his own eternity. The artist stands between the saint and the world of impermanent things, and just in so far as his mind dwells on what is impermanent in his sense, on all that 'modern experience and the discussion of our interests,' that is to say, on what never recurs, as desire and hope, terror and weariness, spring and autumn, recur in varying rhythms, will his mind become critical, as distinguished from creative, and his emotions wither. He will think less of what he sees and more of his own attitude towards it, and will express this attitude by an essentially critical selection and emphasis. I am not quite sure of my memory, but I think that Mr. Ricketts has said in his book on the Prado that he feels the critic in Velasquez for the first time in painting, and we all feel the critic in Whistler and Degas, in Browning, even in Mr. Swinburne, in the finest art of all ages but the greatest. The end for art is the ecstasy awakened by the presence before an ever-changing mind of what is permanent in the world, or by the arousing of that mind itself into the very delicate and fastidious mood habitual with it when it is seeking those permanent and recurring things. There is a little of both ecstasies at all times, but at this time we have a small measure of the creative impulse itself, of the divine vision, a great one of 'the lost traveller's dream under the hill,' perhaps because all the old simple things have been painted or written, and they will only have meaning for us again when a new race or a new civilisation has made us look upon all with new eyesight.

IN THE SERPENT'S MOUTH

There is an old saying that God is a circle whose centre is everywhere. If that is true, the saint goes to the centre, the poet and artist to the ring where everything comes round again. The poet must not seek for what is still and fixed, for that has no life for him; and if he did, his style would become cold and monotonous, and his sense of beauty faint and sickly, as are both style and beauty to my imagination in the prose and poetry of Newman, but be content to find his pleasure in all that is for ever passing away that it may come again, in the beauty of woman, in the fragile flowers of spring, in momentary heroic passion, in whatever is most fleeting, most impassioned, as it were, for its own perfection, most eager to return in its glory. Yet perhaps he must endure the impermanent a little, for these things return, but not wholly, for no two faces are alike, and, it may be, had we more learned eyes, no two flowers. Is it that all things are made by the struggle of the individual and the world, of the unchanging and the returning, and that the saint and the poet are over all, and that the poet has made his home in the Serpent's mouth?

THE BLACK AND THE WHITE ARROWS

Instinct creates the recurring and the beautiful, all the winding of the serpent; but reason, the most ugly man, as Blake called it, is a drawer of the straight line, the maker of the arbitrary and the impermanent, for no recurring spring will ever bring again yesterday's clock. Sanctity has its straight line also, darting from the centre, and with these arrows the many-coloured serpent, theme of all our poetry, is maimed and hunted. He that finds the white arrow shall have wisdom older than the Serpent, but what of the black arrow? How much knowledge, how heavy a quiver of the crow-feathered ebony rods can the soul endure?

HIS MISTRESS'S EYEBROWS

The preoccupation of our Art and Literature with knowledge, with the surface of life, with the arbitrary, with mechanism, has arisen out of the root. A careful but not necessarily very subtle man could foretell the history of any religion if he knew its first principle, and that it would live long enough to fulfil itself. The mind can never do the same thing twice over, and having exhausted simple beauty and meaning, it passes to the strange and hidden, and at last must find its delight, having outrun its harmonies in the emphatic and discordant. When I was a boy at the art school I watched an older student late returned from Paris, with a wonder that had no understanding in it. He was very amorous, and every new love was the occasion of a new picture, and every new picture was uglier than its forerunner. He was excited about his mistress's eyebrows, as was fitting, but the interest of beauty had been exhausted by the logical energies of Art, which destroys where it has rummaged, and can but discover, whether it will or no. We cannot discover our subject matter by deliberate intellect, for when a subject matter ceases to move us we must go elsewhere, and when it moves us, even though it be 'that old ballad material of Shakespeare' or even 'the morbid terror of death,' we can laugh at reason. We must not ask is the world interested in this or that, for nothing is in question but our own interest, and we can understand no other. Our place in the Hierarchy is settled for us by our choice of a subject matter, and all good criticism is hieratic, delighting in setting things above one another, Epic and Drama above Lyric and so on, and not merely side by side. But it is our instinct and not our intellect that chooses. We can deliberately refashion our characters, but not our painting or our poetry. If our characters also were not unconsciously refashioned so completely by the unfolding of the logical energies of Art, that even simple things have in the end a new aspect in our eyes, the Arts would not be among those things that return for ever. The ballads that Bishop Percy gathered returned in the Ancient Mariner and the delight in the world of old Greek sculptors sprang into a more delicate loveliness in that archaistic head of the young athlete down the long corridor to your left hand as you go into the British Museum. Civilisation too, will not that also destroy where it has loved, until it shall bring the simple and natural things again and a new Argo with all the gilding on her bows sail out to find another fleece?

THE TRESSES OF THE HAIR

Hafiz cried to his beloved, 'I made a bargain with that brown hair before the beginning of time, and it shall not be broken through unending time,' and it may be that Mistress Nature knows that we have lived many times, and that whatsoever changes and winds into itself belongs to us. She covers her eyes away from us, but she lets us play with the tresses of her hair.

A TOWER ON THE APENNINES

The other day I was walking towards Urbino, where I was to spend the night, having crossed the Apennines from San Sepolcro, and had come to a level place on the mountain-top near the journey's end. My friends were in a carriage somewhere behind, on a road which was still ascending in great loops, and I was alone amid a visionary, fantastic, impossible scenery. It was sunset and the stormy clouds hung upon mountain after mountain and far off on one great summit a cloud darker than the rest glimmered with lightning. Away south upon another mountain a mediæval tower, with no building near nor any sign of life, rose into the clouds. I saw suddenly in the mind's eye an old man, erect and a little gaunt, standing in the door of the tower, while about him broke a windy light. He was the poet who had at last, because he had done so much for the word's sake, come to share in the dignity of the saint. He had hidden nothing of himself, but he had taken care of 'that dignity ... the perfection of form ... this lofty and severe quality ... this virtue.' And though he had but sought it for the word's sake, or for a woman's praise, it had come at last into his body and his mind. Certainly as he stood there he knew how from behind that laborious mood, that pose, that genius, no flower of himself but all himself, looked out as from behind a mask that other Who alone of all men, the country-people say, is not a hair's breadth more nor less than six feet high. He has in his ears well-instructed voices and seeming solid sights are before his eyes, and not as we say of many a one, speaking in metaphor, but as this were Delphi or Eleusis, and the substance and the voice come to him among his memories which are of women's faces; for was it Columbanus or another that wrote 'There is one among the birds that is perfect, and one perfect among the fish'?

THE THINKING OF THE BODY

Those learned men who are a terror to children and an ignominious sight in lovers' eyes, all those butts of a traditional humour where there is something of the wisdom of peasants, are mathematicians, theologians, lawyers, men of science of various kinds. They have followed some abstract reverie, which stirs the brain only and needs that only, and have therefore stood before the looking-glass without pleasure and never known those thoughts that shape the lines of the body for beauty or animation, and wake a desire for praise or for display.

There are two pictures of Venice side by side in the house where I am writing this, a Canaletto that has little but careful drawing, and a not very emotional pleasure in clean bright air, and a Franz Francken, where the blue water, that in the other stirs one so little, can make one long to plunge into the green depth where a cloud shadow falls. Neither painting could move us at all, if our thought did not rush out to the edges of our flesh, and it is so with all good art, whether the Victory of Samothrace which reminds the soles of our feet of swiftness, or the Odyssey that would send us out under the salt wind, or the young horsemen on the Parthenon, that seem happier than our boyhood ever was, and in our boyhood's way. Art bids us touch and taste and hear and see the world, and shrinks from what Blake calls mathematic form, from every abstract thing, from all that is of the brain only, from all that is not a fountain jetting from the entire hopes, memories, and sensations of the body. Its morality is personal, knows little of any general law, has no blame for Little Musgrave, no care for Lord Barnard's house, seems lighter than a breath and yet is hard and heavy, for if a man is not ready to face toil and risk, and in all gaiety of heart, his body will grow unshapely and his heart lack the wild will that stirs desire. It approved before all men those that talked or wrestled or tilted under the walls of Urbino, or sat in the wide window-seats discussing all things, with love ever in their thought, when the wise Duchess ordered all, and the Lady Emilia gave the theme.

RELIGIOUS BELIEF NECESSARY TO RELIGIOUS ART

All art is sensuous, but when a man puts only his contemplative nature and his more vague desires into his art, the sensuous images through which it speaks become broken, fleeting, uncertain, or are chosen for their distance from general experience, and all grows unsubstantial and fantastic. When imagination moves in a dim world like the country of sleep in Love's Nocturne and 'Siren there winds her dizzy hair and sings,' we go to it for delight indeed but in our weariness. If we are to sojourn there that world must grow consistent with itself, emotion must be related to emotion by a system of ordered images, as in the Divine Comedy. It must grow to be symbolic, that is, for the soul can only achieve a distinct separated life where many related objects at once distinguish and arouse its energies in their fulness. All visionaries have entered into such a world in trances, and all ideal art has trance for warranty. Shelley seemed to Matthew Arnold to beat his ineffectual wings in the void, and I only made my pleasure in him contented pleasure by massing in my imagination his recurring images of towers and rivers, and caves with fountains in them, and that one star of his, till his world had grown solid underfoot and consistent enough for the soul's habitation.

But even then I lacked something to compensate my imagination for geographical and historical reality, for the testimony of our ordinary senses, and found myself wishing for and trying to imagine, as I had also when reading Keats' Endymion, a crowd of believers who could put into all those strange sights the strength of their belief and the rare testimony of their visions. A little crowd had been sufficient, and I would have had Shelley a sectary that his revelation might have found the only sufficient evidence of religion, miracle. All symbolic art should arise out of a real belief, and that it cannot do so in this age proves that this age is a road and not a resting-place for the imaginative arts. I can only understand others by myself, and I am certain that there are many who are not moved as they desire to be by that solitary light burning in the tower of Prince Athanais, because it has not entered into men's prayers nor lighted any through the sacred dark of religious contemplation.

Lyrical poems, when they but speak of emotions common to all, require not indeed a religious belief like the spiritual arts, but a life that has leisure for itself, and a society that is quickly stirred that our emotion may be strengthened by the emotion of others. All circumstance that makes emotion at once dignified and visible, increases the poet's power, and I think that is why I have always longed for some stringed instrument, and a listening audience, not drawn out of the hurried streets, but from a life where it would be natural to murmur over again the singer's thought. When I heard Yvette Guilbert the other day, who has the lyre or as good, I was not content, for she sang among people whose life had nothing it could share with an exquisite art, that should rise out of life as the blade out of the spearshaft, a song out of the mood, the fountain from its pool, all art out of the body, laughter from a happy company. I longed to make all things over again, that she might sing in some great hall, where there was no one that did not love life and speak of it continually.

THE HOLY PLACES

When all art was struck out of personality, whether as in our daily business or in the adventure of religion, there was little separation between holy and common things, and just as the arts themselves passed quickly from passion to divine contemplation, from the conversation of peasants to that of princes, the one song remembering the drunken miller and but half forgetting Cambuscan bold; so did a man feel himself near sacred presences when he turned his plough from the slope of Cruachmaa or of Olympus. The occupations and the places known to Homer or to Hesiod, those pure first artists, might, as it were, if but the fashioners' hands had loosened, have changed before the poem's end to symbols and vanished, winged and unweary, into the unchanging worlds where religion alone can discover life as well as peace. A man of that unbroken day could have all the subtlety of Shelley, and yet use no image unknown among the common people, and speak no thought that was not a deduction from the common thought. Unless the discovery of legendary knowledge and the returning belief in miracle, or what we must needs call so, can bring once more a new belief in the sanctity of common ploughland, and new wonders that reward no difficult ecclesiastical routine but the common, wayward, spirited man, we may never see again a Shelley and a Dickens in the one body, but be broken to the end. We have grown jealous of the body, and we dress it in dull unshapely clothes, that we may cherish aspiration alone. Molière being but the master of common sense lived ever in the common daylight, but Shakespeare could not, and Shakespeare seems to bring us to the very marketplace, when we remember Shelley's dizzy and Landor's calm disdain of usual daily things. And at last we have Villiers de L'Isle-Adam crying in the ecstasy of a supreme culture, of a supreme refusal, 'as for living, our servants will do that for us.' One of the means of loftiness, of marmorean stillness has been the choice of strange and far-away places, for the scenery of art, but this choice has grown bitter to me, and there are moments when I cannot believe in the reality of imaginations that are not inset with the minute life of long familiar things and symbols and places. I have come to think of even Shakespeare's journeys to Rome or to Verona as the outflowing of an unrest, a dissatisfaction with natural interests, an unstable equilibrium of the whole European mind that would not have come had John Palæologus cherished, despite that high and heady look, copied by Burne Jones for his Cophetua, a hearty disposition to fight the Turk. I am orthodox and pray for a resurrection of the body, and am certain that a man should find his Holy Land where he first crept upon the floor, and that familiar woods and rivers should fade into symbol with so gradual a change that he never discover, no, not even in ecstasy itself, that he is beyond space, and that time alone keeps him from Primum Mobile, the Supernal Eden, and the White Rose over all.

1906.

I

When Mr. O'Leary died I could not bring myself to go to his funeral, though I had been once his close fellow-worker, for I shrank from seeing about his grave so many whose Nationalism was different from anything he had taught or that I could share. He belonged, as did his friend John F. Taylor, to the romantic conception of Irish Nationality on which Lionel Johnson and myself founded, so far as it was founded on anything but literature, our Art and our Irish criticism. Perhaps his spirit, if it can care for or can see old friends now, will accept this apology for an absence that has troubled me. I learned much from him and much from Taylor, who will always seem to me the greatest orator I have heard; and that ideal Ireland, perhaps from this out an imaginary Ireland, in whose service I labour, will always be in many essentials their Ireland. They were the last to speak an understanding of life and Nationality, built up by the generation of Grattan, which read Homer and Virgil, and by the generation of Davis, which had been pierced through by the idealism of Mazzini,[2] and of the European revolutionists of the mid-century.

O'Leary had joined the Fenian movement with no hope of success as we know, but because he believed such a movement good for the moral character of the people; and had taken his long imprisonment without complaining. Even to the very end, while often speaking of his prison life, he would have thought it took from his Roman courage to describe its hardship. The worth of a man's acts in the moral memory, a continual height of mind in the doing of them, seemed more to him than their immediate result, if, indeed, the sight of many failures had not taken away the thought of success. A man was not to lie, or even to give up his dignity, on any patriotic plea, and I have heard him say, 'I have but one religion, the old Persian: to bend the bow and tell the truth,' and again, 'There are things a man must not do to save a nation,' and again, 'A man must not cry in public to save a nation,' and that we might not forget justice in the passion of controversy, 'There was never cause so bad that it has not been defended by good men for what seemed to them good reasons.' His friend had a burning and brooding imagination that divided men not according to their achievement but by their degrees of sincerity, and by their mastery over a straight and, to my thought, too obvious logic that seemed to him essential to sincerity. Neither man had an understanding of style or of literature in the right sense of the word, though both were great readers, but because their imagination could come to rest no place short of greatness, they hoped, John O'Leary especially, for an Irish literature of the greatest kind. When Lionel Johnson and Katharine Tynan (as she was then), and I, myself, began to reform Irish poetry, we thought to keep unbroken the thread running up to Grattan which John O'Leary had put into our hands, though it might be our business to explore new paths of the labyrinth. We sought to make a more subtle rhythm, a more organic form, than that of the older Irish poets who wrote in English, but always to remember certain ardent ideas and high attitudes of mind which were the nation itself, to our belief, so far as a nation can be summarised in the intellect. If you had asked an ancient Spartan what made Sparta Sparta, he would have answered, The Laws of Lycurgus, and many Englishmen look back to Bunyan and to Milton as we did to Grattan and to Mitchell. Lionel Johnson was able to take up into his Art one portion of this tradition that I could not, for he had a gift of speaking political thought in fine verse that I have always lacked. I, on the other hand, was more preoccupied with Ireland (for he had other interests), and took from Allingham and Walsh their passion for country spiritism, and from Ferguson his pleasure in heroic legend, and while seeing all in the light of European literature found my symbols of expression in Ireland. One thought often possessed me very strongly. New from the influence, mainly the personal influence, of William Morris, I dreamed of enlarging Irish hate, till we had come to hate with a passion of patriotism what Morris and Ruskin hated. Mitchell had already all but poured some of that hate drawn from Carlyle, who had it of an earlier and, as I think, cruder sort, into the blood of Ireland, and were we not a poor nation with ancient courage, unblackened fields and a barbarous gift of self-sacrifice? Ruskin and Morris had spent themselves in vain because they had found no passion to harness to their thought, but here was unwasted passion and precedents in the popular memory for every needed thought and action. Perhaps, too, it would be possible to find in that new philosophy of spiritism coming to a seeming climax in the work of Fredrick Myers, and in the investigations of uncounted obscure persons, what could change the country spiritism into a reasoned belief that would put its might into all the rest. A new belief seemed coming that could be so simple and demonstrable and above all so mixed into the common scenery of the world, that it would set the whole man on fire and liberate him from a thousand obediences and complexities. We were to forge in Ireland a new sword on our old traditional anvil for that great battle that must in the end re-establish the old, confident, joyous world. All the while I worked with this idea, founding societies that became quickly or slowly everything I despised. One part of me looked on, mischievous and mocking, and the other part spoke words which were more and more unreal, as the attitude of mind became more and more strained and difficult. Madame Maud Gonne could still draw great crowds out of the slums by her beauty and sincerity, and speak to them of 'Mother Ireland with the crown of stars about her head.' But gradually the political movement she was associated with, finding it hard to build up any fine lasting thing, became content to attack little persons and little things. All movements are held together more by what they hate than by what they love, for love separates and individualises and quiets, but the nobler movements, the only movements on which literature can found itself, hate great and lasting things. All who have any old traditions have something of aristocracy, but we had opposing us from the first, though not strongly from the first, a type of mind which had been without influence in the generation of Grattan, and almost without it in that of Davis, and which has made a new nation out of Ireland, that was once old and full of memories.

I remember, when I was twenty years old, arguing, on my way home from a Young Ireland Society, that Ireland, with its hieratic Church, its readiness to accept leadership in intellectual things, and John O'Leary spoke much of this readiness,[3] its Latin hatred of middle paths and uncompleted arguments, could never create a democratic poet of the type of Burns, although it had tried to do so more than once, but that its genius would in the long run be aristocratic and lonely. Whenever I had known some old countryman, I had heard stories and sayings that arose out of an imagination that would have understood Homer better than The Cotter's Saturday Night or Highland Mary, because it was an ancient imagination, where the sediment had found the time to settle, and I believe that the makers of deliberate literature could still take passion and theme, though but little thought, from such as he. On some such old and broken stem, I thought, have all the most beautiful roses been grafted.

II

Him who trembles before the flame and the flood,   And the winds that blow through the starry ways;   Let the starry winds and the flame and the flood   Cover over and hide, for he has no part With the proud, majestical multitude.

Three types of men have made all beautiful things. Aristocracies have made beautiful manners, because their place in the world puts them above the fear of life, and the countrymen have made beautiful stories and beliefs, because they have nothing to lose and so do not fear, and the artists have made all the rest, because Providence has filled them with recklessness. All these look backward to a long tradition, for, being without fear, they have held to whatever pleased them. The others being always anxious have come to possess little that is good in itself, and are always changing from thing to thing, for whatever they do or have must be a means to something else, and they have so little belief that anything can be an end in itself, that they cannot understand you if you say, 'All the most valuable things are useless.' They prefer the stalk to the flower, and believe that painting and poetry exist that there may be instruction, and love that there may be children, and theatres that busy men may rest, and holidays that busy men may go on being busy. At all times they fear and even hate the things that have worth in themselves, for that worth may suddenly, as it were a fire, consume their book of Life, where the world is represented by cyphers and symbols; and before all else, they fear irreverent joy and unserviceable sorrow. It seems to them, that those who have been freed by position, by poverty, or by the traditions of Art, have something terrible about them, a light that is unendurable to eyesight. They complain much of that commandment that we can do almost what we will, if we do it gaily, and think that freedom is but a trifling with the world.

If we would find a company of our own way of thinking, we must go backward to turreted walls, to courts, to high rocky places, to little walled towns, to jesters like that jester of Charles the Fifth who made mirth out of his own death; to the Duke Guidobaldo in his sickness, or Duke Frederick in his strength, to all those who understood that life is not lived, if not lived for contemplation or excitement.

Certainly we could not delight in that so courtly thing, the poetry of light love, if it were sad; for only when we are gay over a thing, and can play with it, do we show ourselves its master, and have minds clear enough for strength. The raging fire and the destructive sword are portions of eternity, too great for the eye of man, wrote Blake, and it is only before such things, before a love like that of Tristan and Iseult, before noble or ennobled death, that the free mind permits itself aught but brief sorrow. That we may be free from all the rest, sullen anger, solemn virtue, calculating anxiety, gloomy suspicion, prevaricating hope, we should be reborn in gaiety. Because there is submission in a pure sorrow, we should sorrow alone over what is greater than ourselves, nor too soon admit that greatness, but all that is less than we are should stir us to some joy, for pure joy masters and impregnates; and so to world end, strength shall laugh and wisdom mourn.

III

In life courtesy and self-possession, and in the arts style, are the sensible impressions of the free mind, for both arise out of a deliberate shaping of all things, and from never being swept away, whatever the emotion, into confusion or dulness. The Japanese have numbered with heroic things courtesy at all times whatsoever, and though a writer, who has to withdraw so much of his thought out of his life that he may learn his craft, may find many his betters in daily courtesy, he should never be without style, which is but high breeding in words and in argument. He is indeed the Creator of the standards of manners in their subtlety, for he alone can know the ancient records and be like some mystic courtier who has stolen the keys from the girdle of time, and can wander where it please him amid the splendours of ancient courts.

Sometimes, it may be, he is permitted the license of cap and bell, or even the madman's bunch of straws, but he never forgets or leaves at home the seal and the signature. He has at all times the freedom of the well-bred, and being bred to the tact of words can take what theme he pleases, unlike the linen drapers, who are rightly compelled to be very strict in their conversation. Who should be free if he were not? for none other has a continual deliberate self-delighting happiness, style, 'the only thing that is immortal in literature,' as Sainte-Beuve has said, a still unexpended energy, after all that the argument or the story need, a still unbroken pleasure after the immediate end has been accomplished, and builds this up into a most personal and wilful fire, transfiguring words and sounds and events. It is the playing of strength when the day's work is done, a secret between a craftsman and his craft, and is so inseparate in his nature, that he has it most of all amid overwhelming emotion, and in the face of death. Shakespeare's persons, when the last darkness has gathered about them, speak out of an ecstasy that is one half the self-surrender of sorrow, and one half the last playing and mockery of the victorious sword, before the defeated world.

It is in the arrangement of events as in the words, and in that touch of extravagance, of irony, of surprise, which is set there after the desire of logic has been satisfied and all that is merely necessary established, and that leaves one, not in the circling necessity, but caught up into the freedom of self-delight: it is, as it were, the foam upon the cup, the long pheasant's feather on the horse's head, the spread peacock over the pasty. If it be very conscious, very deliberate, as it may be in comedy, for comedy is more personal than tragedy, we call it phantasy, perhaps even mischievous phantasy, recognising how disturbing it is to all that drag a ball at the ankle. This joy, because it must be always making and mastering, remains in the hands and in the tongue of the artist, but with his eyes he enters upon a submissive, sorrowful contemplation of the great irremediable things, and he is known from other men by making all he handles like himself, and yet by the unlikeness to himself of all that comes before him in a pure contemplation. It may have been his enemy or his love or his cause that set him dreaming, and certainly the phoenix can but open her young wings in a flaming nest; but all hate and hope vanishes in the dream, and if his mistress brag of the song or his enemy fear it, it is not that either has its praise or blame, but that the twigs of the holy nest are not easily set afire. The verses may make his mistress famous as Helen or give a victory to his cause, not because he has been either's servant, but because men delight to honour and to remember all that have served contemplation. It had been easier to fight, to die even, for Charles's house with Marvel's poem in the memory, but there is no zeal of service that had not been an impurity in the pure soil where the marvel grew. Timon of Athens contemplates his own end, and orders his tomb by the beachy margent of the flood, and Cleopatra sets the asp to her bosom, and their words move us because their sorrow is not their own at tomb or asp, but for all men's fate. That shaping joy has kept the sorrow pure, as it had kept it were the emotion love or hate, for the nobleness of the Arts is in the mingling of contraries, the extremity of sorrow, the extremity of joy, perfection of personality, the perfection of its surrender, overflowing turbulent energy, and marmorean stillness; and its red rose opens at the meeting of the two beams of the cross, and at the trysting-place of mortal and immortal, time and eternity. No new man has ever plucked that rose, or found that trysting-place, for he could but come to the understanding of himself, to the mastery of unlocking words after long frequenting of the great Masters, hardly without ancestral memory of the like. Even knowledge is not enough, for the 'recklessness' Castiglione thought necessary in good manners is necessary in this likewise, and if a man has it not he will be gloomy, and had better to his marketing again.

IV

When I saw John O'Leary first, every young catholic man who had intellectual ambition fed his imagination with the poetry of Young Ireland; and the verses of even the least known of its poets were expounded with a devout ardour at Young Ireland Societies and the like, and their birthdays celebrated. The School of writers I belonged to tried to found itself on much of the subject-matter of this poetry, and, what was almost more in our thoughts, to begin a more imaginative tradition in Irish literature, by a criticism at once remorseless and enthusiastic. It was our criticism, I think, that set Clarence Mangan at the head of the Young Ireland poets in the place of Davis, and put Sir Samuel Ferguson, who had died with but little fame as a poet, next in the succession. Our attacks, mine especially, on verse which owed its position to its moral or political worth, roused a resentment which even I find it hard to imagine to-day, and our verse was attacked in return, and not for anything peculiar to ourselves, but for all that it had in common with the accepted poetry of the world, and most of all for its lack of rhetoric, its refusal to preach a doctrine or to consider the seeming necessities of a cause. Now, after so many years, I can see how natural, how poetical, even, an opposition was, that shows what large numbers could not call up certain high feelings without accustomed verses, or believe we had not wronged the feeling when we did but attack the verses. I have just read in a newspaper that Sir Charles Gavan Duffy recited upon his death bed his favourite poem, one of the worst of the patriotic poems of Young Ireland, and it has brought all this to mind, for the opposition to our School claimed him as its leader. When I was at Siena, I noticed that the Byzantine style persisted in faces of Madonnas for several generations after it had given way to a more natural style, in the less loved faces of saints and martyrs. Passion had grown accustomed to those sloping and narrow eyes, which are almost Japanese, and to those gaunt cheeks, and would have thought it sacrilege to change. We would not, it is likely, have found listeners if John O'Leary, the irreproachable patriot, had not supported us. It was as clear to him that a writer must not write badly, or ignore the examples of the great masters in the fancied or real service of a cause, as it was that he must not lie for it or grow hysterical. I believed in those days that a new intellectual life would begin, like that of Young Ireland, but more profound and personal, and that could we but get a few plain principles accepted, new poets and writers of prose would make an immortal music. I think I was more blind than Johnson, though I judge this from his poems rather than anything I remember of his talk, for he never talked ideas, but, as was common with his generation in Oxford, facts and immediate impressions from life. With others this renunciation was but a pose, a superficial reaction from the disordered abundance of the middle century, but with him it was the radical life. He was in all a traditionalist, gathering out of the past phrases, moods, attitudes, and disliking ideas less for their uncertainty than because they made the mind itself changing and restless. He measured the Irish tradition by another greater than itself, and was quick to feel any falling asunder of the two, yet at many moments they seemed but one in his imagination. Ireland, all through his poem of that name, speaks to him with the voice of the great poets, and in Ireland Dead she is still mother of perfect heroism, but there doubt comes too.

Can it be they do repent That they went, thy chivalry, Those sad ways magnificent?

And in Ways of War, dedicated to John O'Leary, he dismissed the belief in an heroic Ireland as but a dream.

A dream! a dream! an ancient dream! Yet ere peace come to Innisfail, Some weapons on some field must gleam, Some burning glory fire the Gael.

That field may lie beneath the sun, Fair for the treading of an host: That field in realms of thought be won, And armed hands do their uttermost:

Some way, to faithful Innisfail, Shall come the majesty and awe Of martial truth, that must prevail To lay on all the eternal law.

I do not think either of us saw that, as belief in the possibility of armed insurrection withered, the old romantic nationalism would wither too, and that the young would become less ready to find pleasure in whatever they believed to be literature. Poetical tragedy, and indeed all the more intense forms of literature, had lost their hold on the general mass of men in other countries as life grew safe, and the sense of comedy which is the social bond in times of peace as tragic feeling is in times of war, had become the inspiration of popular art. I always knew this, but I believed that the memory of danger, and the reality of it seemed near enough sometimes, would last long enough to give Ireland her imaginative opportunity. I could not foresee that a new class, which had begun to rise into power under the shadow of Parnell, would change the nature of the Irish movement, which, needing no longer great sacrifices, nor bringing any great risk to individuals, could do without exceptional men, and those activities of the mind that are founded on the exceptional moment.[4] John O'Leary had spent much of his thought in an unavailing war with the agrarian party, believing it the root of change, but the fox that crept into the badger's hole did not come from there. Power passed to small shop-keepers, to clerks, to that very class who had seemed to John O'Leary so ready to bend to the power of others, to men who had risen above the traditions of the countryman, without learning those of cultivated life or even educating themselves, and who because of their poverty, their ignorance, their superstitious piety, are much subject to all kinds of fear. Immediate victory, immediate utility, became everything, and the conviction, which is in all who have run great risks for a cause's sake, in the O'Learys and Mazzinis as in all rich natures, that life is greater than the cause, withered, and we artists, who are the servants not of any cause but of mere naked life, and above all of that life in its nobler forms, where joy and sorrow are one, Artificers of the Great Moment, became as elsewhere in Europe protesting individual voices. Ireland's great moment had passed, and she had filled no roomy vessels with strong sweet wine, where we have filled our porcelain jars against the coming winter.

August, 1907.

PREFACE TO THE FIRST EDITION OF JOHN M. SYNGE'S POEMS AND TRANSLATIONS

'The Lonely returns to the Lonely, the Divine to the Divinity.'
Proclus

I

While this work was passing through the press Mr. J. M. Synge died. Upon the morning of his death one friend of his and mine, though away in the country, felt the burden of some heavy event, without understanding where or for whom it was to happen; but upon the same morning one of my sisters said, 'I think Mr. Synge will recover, for last night I dreamed of an ancient galley labouring in a storm and he was in the galley, and suddenly I saw it run into bright sunlight and smooth sea, and I heard the keel grate upon the sand.' The misfortune was for the living certainly, that must work on, perhaps in vain, to magnify the minds and hearts of our young men, and not for the dead that, having cast off the ailing body, is now, as I believe, all passionate and fiery, an heroical thing. Our Daimon is as dumb as was that of Socrates, when they brought in the hemlock; and if we speak among ourselves, it is of the thoughts that have no savour because we cannot hear his laughter, of the work more difficult because of the strength he has taken with him, of the astringent joy and hardness that was in all he did, and of his fame in the world.

II

In his Preface he speaks of these poems as having been written during the last sixteen or seventeen years, though the greater number were written very recently, and many during his last illness. An Epitaph and On an Anniversary show how early the expectation of death came to him, for they were made long ago. But the book as a whole is a farewell, written when life began to slip from him. He was a reserved man, and wished no doubt by a vague date to hide when still living what he felt and thought, from those about him. I asked one of the nurses in the hospital where he died if he knew he was dying, and she said, 'He may have known it for months, but he would not have spoken of it to anyone.' Even the translations of poems that he has made his own by putting them into that melancholy dialect of his, seem to express his emotion at the memory of poverty and the approach of death. The whole book is of a kind almost unknown in a time when lyricism has become abstract and impersonal.

III

Now and then in history some man will speak a few simple sentences which never die, because his life gives them energy and meaning. They affect us as do the last words of Shakespeare's people that gather up into themselves the energy of elaborate events, and they in their turn put strange meaning into half-forgotten things and accidents, like cries that reveal the combatants in some dim battle. Often a score of words will be enough, as when we repeat to ourselves, 'I am a servant of the Lord God of War and I understand the lovely art of the Muses,' all that remains of a once famous Greek poet and sea rover. And is not that epitaph Swift made in Latin for his own tomb more immortal than his pamphlets, perhaps than his great allegory? 'He has gone where fierce indignation will lacerate his heart no more.' I think this book too has certain sentences, fierce or beautiful or melancholy that will be remembered in our history, having behind their passion his quarrel with ignorance, and those passionate events, his books.

But for the violent nature that strikes brief fire in A Question, hidden though it was under much courtesy and silence, his genius had never borne those lion cubs of his. He could not have loved had he not hated, nor honoured had he not scorned; though his hatred and his scorn moved him but seldom, as I think, for his whole nature was lifted up into a vision of the world, where hatred played with the grotesque and love became an ecstatic contemplation of noble life.

He once said to me, 'We must unite asceticism, stoicism, ecstasy; two of these have often come together, but not all three:' and the strength that made him delight in setting the hard virtues by the soft, the bitter by the sweet, salt by mercury, the stone by the elixir, gave him a hunger for harsh facts, for ugly surprising things, for all that defies our hope. In The Passing of the Shee he is repelled by the contemplation of a beauty too far from life to appease his mood; and in his own work, benign images ever present to his soul must have beside them malignant reality, and the greater the brightness, the greater must the darkness be. Though like 'Usheen after the Fenians' he remembers his master and his friends, he cannot put from his mind coughing and old age and the sound of the bells. The old woman in The Riders to the Sea, in mourning for her six fine sons, mourns for the passing of all beauty and strength, while the drunken woman of The Tinker's Wedding is but the more drunken and the more thieving because she can remember great queens. And what is it but desire of ardent life, like that of Usheen for his 'golden salmon of the sea, cleen hawk of the air,' that makes the young girls of The Playboy of the Western World prefer to any peaceful man their eyes have looked upon, a seeming murderer? Person after person in these laughing, sorrowful, heroic plays is, 'the like of the little children do be listening to the stories of an old woman, and do be dreaming after in the dark night it's in grand houses of gold they are, with speckled horses to ride, and do be waking again in a short while and they destroyed with the cold, and the thatch dripping, maybe, and the starved ass braying in the yard.'

IV

It was only at the last in his unfinished Deirdre of the Sorrows that his mood changed. He knew some twelve months ago that he was dying, though he told no one about it but his betrothed, and he gave all his thought to this play, that he might finish it. Sometimes he would despond and say that he could not; and then his betrothed would act it for him in his sick room, and give him heart to write again. And now by a strange chance, for he began the play before the last failing of his health, his persons awake to no disillusionment but to death only, and as if his soul already thirsted for the fiery fountains there is nothing grotesque, but beauty only.

V

He was a solitary, undemonstrative man, never asking pity, nor complaining, nor seeking sympathy but in this book's momentary cries: all folded up in brooding intellect, knowing nothing of new books and newspapers, reading the great masters alone; and he was but the more hated because he gave his country what it needed, an unmoved mind where there is a perpetual last day, a trumpeting, and coming up to judgment.

April 4, 1909.

J. M. SYNGE AND THE IRELAND OF HIS TIME

I

On Saturday, January 26th, 1907, I was lecturing in Aberdeen, and when my lecture was over I was given a telegram which said, 'Play great success.' It had been sent from Dublin after the second act of The Playboy of the Western World, then being performed for the first time. After one in the morning, my host brought to my bedroom this second telegram, 'Audience broke up in disorder at the word shift.' I knew no more until I got the Dublin papers on my way from Belfast to Dublin on Tuesday morning. On the Monday night no word of the play had been heard. About forty young men had sat on the front seats of the pit, and stamped and shouted and blown trumpets from the rise to the fall of the curtain. On the Tuesday night also the forty young men were there. They wished to silence what they considered a slander upon Ireland's womanhood. Irish women would never sleep under the same roof with a young man without a chaperon, nor admire a murderer, nor use a word like 'shift'; nor could anyone recognise the countrymen and women of Davis and Kickham in these poetical, violent, grotesque persons, who used the name of God so freely, and spoke of all things that hit their fancy.

A patriotic journalism which had seen in Synge's capricious imagination the enemy of all it would have young men believe, had for years prepared for this hour, by that which is at once the greatest and most ignoble power of journalism, the art of repeating a name again and again with some ridiculous or evil association. The preparation had begun after the first performance of The Shadow of the Glen, Synge's first play, with an assertion made in ignorance but repeated in dishonesty, that he had taken his fable and his characters, not from his own mind nor that profound knowledge of cot and curragh he was admitted to possess, but 'from a writer of the Roman decadence.' Some spontaneous dislike had been but natural, for genius like his can but slowly, amid what it has of harsh and strange, set forth the nobility of its beauty, and the depth of its compassion; but the frenzy that would have silenced his master-work was, like most violent things artificial, the defence of virtue by those that have but little, which is the pomp and gallantry of journalism and its right to govern the world.

As I stood there watching, knowing well that I saw the dissolution of a school of patriotism that held sway over my youth, Synge came and stood beside me, and said, 'A young doctor has just told me that he can hardly keep himself from jumping on to a seat, and pointing out in that howling mob those whom he is treating for venereal disease.'

II

Thomas Davis, whose life had the moral simplicity which can give to actions the lasting influence that style alone can give to words, had understood that a country which has no national institutions must show its young men images for the affections, although they be but diagrams of what it should be or may be. He and his school imagined the Soldier, the Orator, the Patriot, the Poet, the Chieftain, and above all the Peasant; and these, as celebrated in essay and songs and stories, possessed so many virtues that no matter how England, who, as Mitchell said, 'had the ear of the world,' might slander us, Ireland, even though she could not come at the world's other ear, might go her way unabashed. But ideas and images which have to be understood and loved by large numbers of people, must appeal to no rich personal experience, no patience of study, no delicacy of sense; and if at rare moments some Memory of the Dead can take its strength from one; at all other moments manner and matter will be rhetorical, conventional, sentimental; and language, because it is carried beyond life perpetually, will be as wasted as the thought, with unmeaning pedantries and silences, and a dread of all that has salt and savour. After a while, in a land that has given itself to agitation over-much, abstract thoughts are raised up between men's minds and Nature, who never does the same thing twice, or makes one man like another, till minds, whose patriotism is perhaps great enough to carry them to the scaffold, cry down natural impulse with the morbid persistence of minds unsettled by some fixed idea. They are preoccupied with the nation's future, with heroes, poets, soldiers, painters, armies, fleets, but only as these things are understood by a child in a national school, while a secret feeling that what is so unreal needs continual defence makes them bitter and restless. They are like some state which has only paper money, and seeks by punishments to make it buy whatever gold can buy. They no longer love, for only life is loved, and at last, a generation is like an hysterical woman who will make unmeasured accusations and believe impossible things, because of some logical deduction from a solitary thought which has turned a portion of her mind to stone.

III

Even if what one defends be true, an attitude of defence, a continual apology, whatever the cause, makes the mind barren because it kills intellectual innocence; that delight in what is unforeseen, and in the mere spectacle of the world, the mere drifting hither and thither that must come before all true thought and emotion. A zealous Irishman, especially if he lives much out of Ireland, spends his time in a never-ending argument about Oliver Cromwell, the Danes, the penal laws, the rebellion of 1798, the famine, the Irish peasant, and ends by substituting a traditional casuistry for a country; and if he be a Catholic, yet another casuistry that has professors, schoolmasters, letter-writing priests and the authors of manuals to make the meshes fine, comes between him and English literature, substituting arguments and hesitations for the excitement at the first reading of the great poets which should be a sort of violent imaginative puberty. His hesitations and arguments may have been right, the Catholic philosophy may be more profound than Milton's morality, or Shelley's vehement vision; but none the less do we lose life by losing that recklessness Castiglione thought necessary even in good manners, and offend our Lady Truth, who would never, had she desired an anxious courtship, have digged a well to be her parlour.

I admired, though we were always quarrelling, J. F. Taylor, the orator, who died just before the first controversy over these plays. It often seemed to me that when he spoke Ireland herself had spoken, one got that sense of surprise that comes when a man has said what is unforeseen because it is far from the common thought, and yet obvious because when it has been spoken, the gate of the mind seems suddenly to roll back and reveal forgotten sights and let loose lost passions. I have never heard him speak except in some Irish literary or political society, but there at any rate, as in conversation, I found a man whose life was a ceaseless reverie over the religious and political history of Ireland. He saw himself pleading for his country before an invisible jury, perhaps of the great dead, against traitors at home and enemies abroad, and a sort of frenzy in his voice and the moral elevation of his thoughts gave him for the moment style and music. One asked oneself again and again, 'Why is not this man an artist, a man of genius, a creator of some kind?' The other day under the influence of memory, I read through his one book, a life of Owen Roe O'Neill, and found there no sentence detachable from its context because of wisdom or beauty. Everything was argued from a premise; and wisdom and style, whether in life or letters, come from the presence of what is self-evident, from that which requires but statement, from what Blake called 'naked beauty displayed.'

The sense of what was unforeseen and obvious, the rolling backward of the gates, had gone with the living voice, with the nobility of will that made one understand what he saw and felt in what was now but argument and logic. I found myself in the presence of a mind like some noisy and powerful machine, of thought that was no part of wisdom but the apologetic of a moment, a woven thing, no intricacy of leaf and twig, of words with no more of salt and of savour than those of a Jesuit professor of literature, or of any other who does not know that there is no lasting writing which does not define the quality, or carry the substance of some pleasure. How can one, if one's mind be full of abstractions and images created not for their own sake but for the sake of party, even if there were still the need, make pictures for the mind's eye and sounds that delight the ear, or discover thoughts that tighten the muscles, or quiver and tingle in the flesh, and so stand like St. Michael with the trumpet that calls the body to resurrection?

IV

Young Ireland had taught a study of our history with the glory of Ireland for event, and this for lack, when less than Taylor studied, of comparison with that of other countries wrecked the historical instinct. An old man with an academic appointment, who was a leader in the attack upon Synge sees in the eleventh century romance of Deirdre a retelling of the first five-act tragedy outside the classic languages, and this tragedy from his description of it was certainly written on the Elizabethan model; while an allusion to a copper boat, a marvel of magic like Cinderella's slipper, persuades him that the ancient Irish had forestalled the modern dockyards in the making of metal ships. The man who doubted, let us say, our fabulous ancient kings running up to Adam, or found but mythology in some old tale, was as hated as if he had doubted the authority of Scripture. Above all no man was so ignorant, that he had not by rote familiar arguments and statistics to drive away amid familiar applause all those had they but found strange truth in the world or in their mind, whose knowledge has passed out of memory and become an instinct of hand or eye. There was no literature, for literature is a child of experience always, of knowledge never; and the nation itself, instead of being a dumb struggling thought seeking a mouth to utter it or hand to show it, a teeming delight that would re-create the world, had become, at best, a subject of knowledge.

V

Taylor always spoke with confidence, though he was no determined man, being easily flattered or jostled from his way; and this, putting as it were his fiery heart into his mouth, made him formidable. And I have noticed that all those who speak the thoughts of many, speak confidently, while those who speak their own thoughts are hesitating and timid, as though they spoke out of a mind and body grown sensitive to the edge of bewilderment among many impressions. They speak to us that we may give them certainty, by seeing what they have seen; and so it is, that enlargement of experience does not come from those oratorical thinkers, or from those decisive rhythms that move large numbers of men, but from writers that seem by contrast as feminine as the soul when it explores in Blake's picture the recesses of the grave, carrying its faint lamp trembling and astonished; or as the Muses who are never pictured as one-breasted Amazons, but as women needing protection. Indeed, all art which appeals to individual man and awaits the confirmation of his senses and his reveries, seems when arrayed against the moral zeal, the confident logic, the ordered proof of journalism, a trifling, impertinent, vexatious thing, a tumbler who has unrolled his carpet in the way of a marching army.

VI

I attack things that are as dear to many as some holy image carried hither and thither by some broken clan, and can but say that I have felt in my body the affections I disturb, and believed that if I could raise them into contemplation I would make possible a literature, that, finding its subject-matter all ready in men's minds, would be, not as ours is, an interest for scholars, but the possession of a people. I have founded societies with this aim, and was indeed founding one in Paris when I first met with J. M. Synge, and I have known what it is to be changed by that I would have changed, till I became argumentative and unmannerly, hating men even in daily life for their opinions. And though I was never convinced that the anatomies of last year's leaves are a living forest, nor thought a continual apologetic could do other than make the soul a vapour and the body a stone; nor believed that literature can be made by anything but by what is still blind and dumb within ourselves, I have had to learn how hard in one who lives where forms of expression and habits of thought have been born, not for the pleasure of begetting but for the public good, is that purification from insincerity, vanity, malignity, arrogance, which is the discovery of style. But it became possible to live when I had learnt all I had not learnt in shaping words, in defending Synge against his enemies, and knew that rich energies, fine, turbulent or gracious thoughts, whether in life or letters, are but love-children.

Synge seemed by nature unfitted to think a political thought, and with the exception of one sentence, spoken when I first met him in Paris, that implied some sort of nationalist conviction, I cannot remember that he spoke of politics or showed any interest in men in the mass, or in any subject that is studied through abstractions and statistics. Often for months together he and I and Lady Gregory would see no one outside the Abbey Theatre, and that life, lived as it were in a ship at sea, suited him, for unlike those whose habit of mind fits them to judge of men in the mass, he was wise in judging individual men, and as wise in dealing with them as the faint energies of ill-health would permit; but of their political thoughts he long understood nothing. One night when we were still producing plays in a little hall, certain members of the Company told him that a play on the Rebellion of '98 would be a great success. After a fortnight he brought them a scenario which read like a chapter out of Rabelais. Two women, a Protestant and a Catholic, take refuge in a cave, and there quarrel about religion, abusing the Pope or Queen Elizabeth and Henry VIII, but in low voices, for the one fears to be ravished by the soldiers, the other by the rebels. At last one woman goes out because she would sooner any fate than such wicked company. Yet, I doubt if he would have written at all if he did not write of Ireland, and for it, and I know that he thought creative art could only come from such preoccupation. Once, when in later years, anxious about the educational effect of our movement, I proposed adding to the Abbey Company a second Company to play international drama, Synge, who had not hitherto opposed me, thought the matter so important that he did so in a formal letter.

I had spoken of a German municipal theatre as my model, and he said that the municipal theatres all over Europe gave fine performances of old classics, but did not create (he disliked modern drama for its sterility of speech, and perhaps ignored it), and that we would create nothing if we did not give all our thoughts to Ireland. Yet in Ireland he loved only what was wild in its people, and in 'the grey and wintry sides of many glens.' All the rest, all that one reasoned over, fought for, read of in leading articles, all that came from education, all that came down from Young Ireland, though for this he had not lacked a little sympathy, first wakened in him perhaps that irony which runs through all he wrote, but once awakened, he made it turn its face upon the whole of life. The women quarrelling in the cave would not have amused him, if something in his nature had not looked out on most disputes, even those wherein he himself took sides, with a mischievous wisdom. He told me once that when he lived in some peasant's house, he tried to make those about him forget that he was there, and it is certain that he was silent in any crowded room. It is possible that low vitality helped him to be observant and contemplative, and made him dislike, even in solitude, those thoughts which unite us to others, much as we all dislike, when fatigue or illness has sharpened the nerves, hoardings covered with advertisements, the fronts of big theatres, big London hotels, and all architecture which has been made to impress the crowd. What blindness did for Homer, lameness for Hephæstus, asceticism for any saint you will, bad health did for him by making him ask no more of life than that it should keep him living, and above all perhaps by concentrating his imagination upon one thought, health itself. I think that all noble things are the result of warfare; great nations and classes, of warfare in the visible world, great poetry and philosophy, of invisible warfare, the division of a mind within itself, a victory, the sacrifice of a man to himself. I am certain that my friend's noble art, so full of passion and heroic beauty, is the victory of a man who in poverty and sickness created from the delight of expression, and in the contemplation that is born of the minute and delicate arrangement of images, happiness, and health of mind. Some early poems have a morbid melancholy, and he himself spoke of early work he had destroyed as morbid, for as yet the craftsmanship was not fine enough to bring the artist's joy which is of one substance with that of sanctity. In one poem he waits at some street corner for a friend, a woman perhaps, and while he waits and gradually understands that nobody is coming, sees two funerals and shivers at the future; and in another written on his twenty-fifth birthday, he wonders if the twenty-five years to come shall be as evil as those gone by. Later on, he can see himself as but a part of the spectacle of the world and mix into all he sees that flavour of extravagance, or of humour, or of philosophy, that makes one understand that he contemplates even his own death as if it were another's and finds in his own destiny but as it were a projection through a burning glass of that general to men. There is in the creative joy an acceptance of what life brings, because we have understood the beauty of what it brings, or a hatred of death for what it takes away, which arouses within us, through some sympathy perhaps with all other men, an energy so noble, so powerful, that we laugh aloud and mock, in the terror or the sweetness of our exaltation, at death and oblivion.

In no modern writer that has written of Irish life before him, except it may be Miss Edgeworth in Castle Rackrent, was there anything to change a man's thought about the world or stir his moral nature, for they but play with pictures, persons and events, that whether well or ill observed are but an amusement for the mind where it escapes from meditation, a child's show that makes the fables of his art as significant by contrast as some procession painted on an Egyptian wall; for in these fables, an intelligence, on which the tragedy of the world had been thrust in so few years, that Life had no time to brew her sleepy drug, has spoken of the moods that are the expression of its wisdom. All minds that have a wisdom come of tragic reality seem morbid to those that are accustomed to writers who have not faced reality at all; just as the saints, with that Obscure Night of the Soul, which fell so certainly that they numbered it among spiritual states, one among other ascending steps, seem morbid to the rationalist and the old-fashioned Protestant controversialist. The thought of journalists, like that of the Irish novelists, is neither healthy nor unhealthy, for it has not risen to that state where either is possible, nor should we call it happy; for who would have sought happiness, if happiness were not the supreme attainment of man, in heroic toils, in the cell of the ascetic, or imagined it above the cheerful newspapers, above the clouds?

VII

Not that Synge brought out of the struggle with himself any definite philosophy, for philosophy in the common meaning of the word is created out of an anxiety for sympathy or obedience, and he was that rare, that distinguished, that most noble thing, which of all things still of the world is nearest to being sufficient to itself, the pure artist. Sir Philip Sidney complains of those who could hear 'sweet tunes' (by which he understands could look upon his lady) and not be stirred to 'ravishing delight.'

'Or if they do delight therein, yet are so closed with wit,   As with sententious lips to set a title vain on it; Oh let them hear these sacred tunes, and learn in Wonder's schools   To be, in things past bonds of wit, fools if they be not fools!'

Ireland for three generations has been like those churlish logicians. Everything is argued over, everything has to take its trial before the dull sense and the hasty judgment, and the character of the nation has so changed that it hardly keeps but among country people, or where some family tradition is still stubborn, those lineaments that made Borrow cry out as he came from among the Irish monks, his friends and entertainers for all his Spanish Bible scattering, 'Oh, Ireland, mother of the bravest soldiers and of the most beautiful women!' It was, as I believe, to seek that old Ireland which took its mould from the duellists and scholars of the eighteenth century and from generations older still, that Synge returned again and again to Aran, to Kerry, and to the wild Blaskets.

VIII

'When I got up this morning,' he writes, after he had been a long time in Innismaan, 'I found that the people had gone to Mass and latched the kitchen door from the outside, so that I could not open it to give myself light.

'I sat for nearly an hour beside the fire with a curious feeling that I should be quite alone in this little cottage. I am so used to sitting here with the people that I have never felt the room before as a place where any man might live and work by himself. After a while as I waited, with just light enough from the chimney to let me see the rafters and the greyness of the walls, I became indescribably mournful, for I felt that this little corner on the face of the world, and the people who live in it, have a peace and dignity from which we are shut for ever.' This life, which he describes elsewhere as the most primitive left in Europe, satisfied some necessity of his nature. Before I met him in Paris he had wandered over much of Europe, listening to stories in the Black Forest, making friends with servants and with poor people, and this from an æsthetic interest, for he had gathered no statistics, had no money to give, and cared nothing for the wrongs of the poor, being content to pay for the pleasure of eye and ear with a tune upon the fiddle. He did not love them the better because they were poor and miserable, and it was only when he found Innismaan and the Blaskets, where there is neither riches nor poverty, neither what he calls 'the nullity of the rich' nor 'the squalor of the poor' that his writing lost its old morbid brooding, that he found his genius and his peace. Here were men and women who under the weight of their necessity lived, as the artist lives, in the presence of death and childhood, and the great affections and the orgiastic moment when life outleaps its limits, and who, as it is always with those who have refused or escaped the trivial and the temporary, had dignity and good manners where manners mattered. Here above all was silence from all our great orator took delight in, from formidable men, from moral indignation, from the 'sciolist' who 'is never sad,' from all in modern life that would destroy the arts; and here, to take a thought from another playwright of our school, he could love Time as only women and great artists do and need never sell it.

IX

As I read The Aran Islands right through for the first time since he showed it me in manuscript, I come to understand how much knowledge of the real life of Ireland went to the creation of a world which is yet as fantastic as the Spain of Cervantes. Here is the story of The Playboy, of The Shadow of the Glen; here is the ghost on horseback and the finding of the young man's body of Riders to the Sea, numberless ways of speech and vehement pictures that had seemed to owe nothing to observation, and all to some overflowing of himself, or to some mere necessity of dramatic construction. I had thought the violent quarrels of The Well of the Saints came from his love of bitter condiments, but here is a couple that quarrel all day long amid neighbours who gather as for a play. I had defended the burning of Christy Mahon's leg on the ground that an artist need but make his characters self-consistent, and yet, that too was observation, for 'although these people are kindly towards each other and their children, they have no sympathy for the suffering of animals, and little sympathy for pain when the person who feels it is not in danger.' I had thought it was in the wantonness of fancy Martin Dhoul accused the smith of plucking his living ducks, but a few lines farther on, in this book where moral indignation is unknown, I read, 'Sometimes when I go into a cottage, I find all the women of the place down on their knees plucking the feathers from live ducks and geese.'

He loves all that has edge, all that is salt in the mouth, all that is rough to the hand, all that heightens the emotions by contest, all that stings into life the sense of tragedy; and in this book, unlike the plays where nearness to his audience moves him to mischief, he shows it without thought of other taste than his. It is so constant, it is all set out so simply, so naturally, that it suggests a correspondence between a lasting mood of the soul and this life that shares the harshness of rocks and wind. The food of the spiritual-minded is sweet, an Indian scripture says, but passionate minds love bitter food. Yet he is no indifferent observer, but is certainly kind and sympathetic to all about him. When an old and ailing man, dreading the coming winter, cries at his leaving, not thinking to see him again; and he notices that the old man's mitten has a hole in it where the palm is accustomed to the stick, one knows that it is with eyes full of interested affection as befits a simple man and not in the curiosity of study. When he had left the Blaskets for the last time, he travelled with a lame pensioner who had drifted there, why heaven knows, and one morning having missed him from the inn where they were staying, he believed he had gone back to the island, and searched everywhere and questioned everybody, till he understood of a sudden that he was jealous as though the island were a woman.

The book seems dull if you read much at a time, as the later Kerry essays do not, but nothing that he has written recalls so completely to my senses the man as he was in daily life; and as I read, there are moments when every line of his face, every inflection of his voice, grows so clear in memory that I cannot realise that he is dead. He was no nearer when we walked and talked than now while I read these unarranged, unspeculating pages, wherein the only life he loved with his whole heart reflects itself as in the still water of a pool. Thought comes to him slowly, and only after long seemingly unmeditative watching, and when it comes (and he had the same character in matters of business), it is spoken without hesitation and never changed. His conversation was not an experimental thing, an instrument of research, and this made him silent; while his essays recall events, on which one feels that he pronounces no judgment even in the depth of his own mind, because the labour of Life itself had not yet brought the philosophic generalisation, which was almost as much his object as the emotional generalisation of beauty. A mind that generalises rapidly, continually prevents the experience that would have made it feel and see deeply, just as a man whose character is too complete in youth seldom grows into any energy of moral beauty. Synge had indeed no obvious ideals, as these are understood by young men, and even as I think disliked them, for he once complained to me that our modern poetry was but the poetry 'of the lyrical boy,' and this lack makes his art have a strange wildness and coldness, as of a man born in some far-off spacious land and time.

X

There are artists like Byron, like Goethe, like Shelley, who have impressive personalities, active wills and all their faculties at the service of the will; but he belonged to those who like Wordsworth, like Coleridge, like Goldsmith, like Keats, have little personality, so far as the casual eye can see, little personal will, but fiery and brooding imagination. I cannot imagine him anxious to impress, or convince in any company, or saying more than was sufficient to keep the talk circling. Such men have the advantage that all they write is a part of knowledge, but they are powerless before events and have often but one visible strength, the strength to reject from life and thought all that would mar their work, or deafen them in the doing of it; and only this so long as it is a passive act. If Synge had married young or taken some profession, I doubt if he would have written books or been greatly interested in a movement like ours; but he refused various opportunities of making money in what must have been an almost unconscious preparation. He had no life outside his imagination, little interest in anything that was not its chosen subject. He hardly seemed aware of the existence of other writers. I never knew if he cared for work of mine, and do not remember that I had from him even a conventional compliment, and yet he had the most perfect modesty and simplicity in daily intercourse, self-assertion was impossible to him. On the other hand, he was useless amidst sudden events. He was much shaken by the Playboy riot; on the first night confused and excited, knowing not what to do, and ill before many days, but it made no difference in his work. He neither exaggerated out of defiance nor softened out of timidity. He wrote on as if nothing had happened, altering The Tinker's Wedding to a more unpopular form, but writing a beautiful serene Deirdre, with, for the first time since his Riders to the Sea, no touch of sarcasm or defiance. Misfortune shook his physical nature while it left his intellect and his moral nature untroubled. The external self, the mask, the persona, was a shadow, character was all.

XI

He was a drifting silent man full of hidden passion, and loved wild islands, because there, set out in the light of day, he saw what lay hidden in himself. There is passage after passage in which he dwells upon some moment of excitement. He describes the shipping of pigs at Kilronan on the North Island for the English market: 'when the steamer was getting near, the whole drove was moved down upon the slip and the curraghs were carried out close to the sea. Then each beast was caught in its turn and thrown on its side, while its legs were hitched together in a single knot, with a tag of rope remaining, by which it could be carried.

'Probably the pain inflicted was not great, yet the animals shut their eyes and shrieked with almost human intonations, till the suggestion of the noise became so intense that the men and women who were merely looking on grew wild with excitement, and the pigs waiting their turn foamed at the mouth and tore each other with their teeth.

'After a while there was a pause. The whole slip was covered with a mass of sobbing animals, with here and there a terrified woman crouching among the bodies and patting some special favourite, to keep it quiet while the curraghs were being launched. Then the screaming began again while the pigs were carried out and laid in their places, with a waistcoat tied round their feet to keep them from damaging the canvas. They seemed to know where they were going, and looked up at me over the gunnel with an ignoble desperation that made me shudder to think that I had eaten this whimpering flesh. When the last curragh went out, I was left on the slip with a band of women and children, and one old boar who sat looking out over the sea.

'The women were over-excited, and when I tried to talk to them they crowded round me and began jeering and shrieking at me because I am not married. A dozen screamed at a time, and so rapidly that I could not understand all they were saying, yet I was able to make out that they were taking advantage of the absence of their husbands to give me the full volume of their contempt. Some little boys who were listening threw themselves down, writhing with laughter among the seaweed, and the young girls grew red and embarrassed and stared down in the surf.' The book is full of such scenes. Now it is a crowd going by train to the Parnell celebration, now it is a woman cursing her son who made himself a spy for the police, now it is an old woman keening at a funeral. Kindred to his delight in the harsh grey stones, in the hardship of the life there, in the wind and in the mist, there is always delight in every moment of excitement, whether it is but the hysterical excitement of the women over the pigs, or some primary passion. Once indeed, the hidden passion instead of finding expression by its choice among the passions of others shows itself in the most direct way of all, that of dream. 'Last night,' he writes, at Innismaan, 'after walking in a dream among buildings with strangely intense light on them, I heard a faint rhythm of music beginning far away on some stringed instrument.

'It came closer to me, gradually increasing in quickness and volume with an irresistibly definite progression. When it was quite near the sound began to move in my nerves and blood, to urge me to dance with them.

'I knew that if I yielded I would be carried away into some moment of terrible agony, so I struggled to remain quiet, holding my knees together with my hands.

'The music increased continually, sounding like the strings of harps tuned to a forgotten scale, and having a resonance as searching as the strings of the 'cello.

'Then the luring excitement became more powerful than my will, and my limbs moved in spite of me.

'In a moment I swept away in a whirlwind of notes. My breath and my thoughts and every impulse of my body became a form of the dance, till I could not distinguish between the instrument or the rhythm and my own person or consciousness.

'For a while it seemed an excitement that was filled with joy; then it grew into an ecstasy where all existence was lost in the vortex of movement. I could not think that there had been a life beyond the whirling of the dance.

'Then with a shock, the ecstasy turned to agony and rage. I struggled to free myself but seemed only to increase the passion of the steps I moved to. When I shrieked I could only echo the notes of the rhythm.

'At last, with a movement of uncontrollable frenzy I broke back to consciousness and awoke.

'I dragged myself trembling to the window of the cottage and looked out. The moon was glittering across the bay and there was no sound anywhere on the island.'

XII

In all drama which would give direct expression to reverie, to the speech of the soul with itself, there is some device that checks the rapidity of dialogue. When Oedipus speaks out of the most vehement passions, he is conscious of the presence of the chorus, men before whom he must keep up appearances, 'children latest born of Cadmus' line' who do not share his passion. Nobody is hurried or breathless. We listen to reports and discuss them, taking part as it were in a council of state. Nothing happens before our eyes. The dignity of Greek drama, and in a lesser degree of that of Corneille and Racine, depends, as contrasted with the troubled life of Shakespearean drama, on an almost even speed of dialogue, and on a so continuous exclusion of the animation of common life, that thought remains lofty and language rich. Shakespeare, upon whose stage everything may happen, even the blinding of Gloster, and who has no formal check except what is implied in the slow, elaborate structure of blank verse, obtains time for reverie by an often encumbering Euphuism, and by such a loosening of his plot as will give his characters the leisure to look at life from without. Maeterlinck, to name the first modern of the old way who comes to mind, reaches the same end, by choosing instead of human beings persons who are as faint as a breath upon a looking-glass, symbols who can speak a language slow and heavy with dreams because their own life is but a dream. Modern drama, on the other hand, which accepts the tightness of the classic plot, while expressing life directly, has been driven to make indirect its expression of the mind, which it leaves to be inferred from some common-place sentence or gesture as we infer it in ordinary life; and this is, I believe, the cause of the perpetual disappointment of the hope imagined this hundred years that France or Spain or Germany or Scandinavia will at last produce the master we await.

The divisions in the arts are almost all in the first instance technical, and the great schools of drama have been divided from one another by the form or the metal of their mirror, by the check chosen for the rapidity of dialogue. Synge found the check that suited his temperament in an elaboration of the dialects of Kerry and Aran. The cadence is long and meditative, as befits the thought of men who are much alone, and who when they meet in one another's houses, as their way is at the day's end, listen patiently, each man speaking in turn and for some little time, and taking pleasure in the vaguer meaning of the words and in their sound. Their thought, when not merely practical, is as full of traditional wisdom and extravagant pictures as that of some Æschylean chorus, and no matter what the topic is, it is as though the present were held at arm's length. It is the reverse of rhetoric, for the speaker serves his own delight, though doubtless he would tell you that like Raftery's whiskey-drinking it was but for the company's sake. A medicinal manner of speech too, for it could not even express, so little abstract it is and so rammed with life, those worn generalisations of national propaganda. 'I'll be telling you the finest story you'd hear any place from Dundalk to Ballinacree with great queens in it, making themselves matches from the start to the end, and they with shiny silks on them.... I've a grand story of the great queens of Ireland, with white necks on them the like of Sarah Casey, and fine arms would hit you a slap.... What good am I this night, God help me? What good are the grand stories I have when it's few would listen to an old woman, few but a girl maybe would be in great fear the time her hour was come, or little child wouldn't be sleeping with the hunger on a cold night.' That has the flavour of Homer, of the Bible, of Villon, while Cervantes would have thought it sweet in the mouth though not his food. This use of Irish dialect for noble purpose by Synge, and by Lady Gregory, who had it already in her Cuchulain of Muirthemne, and by Dr. Hyde in those first translations he has not equalled since, has done much for National dignity. When I was a boy I was often troubled and sorrowful because Scottish dialect was capable of noble use, but the Irish of obvious roystering humour only; and this error fixed on my imagination by so many novelists and rhymers made me listen badly. Synge wrote down words and phrases wherever he went, and with that knowledge of Irish which made all our country idioms easy to his hand, found it so rich a thing, that he had begun translating into it fragments of the great literatures of the world, and had planned a complete version of The Imitation of Christ. It gave him imaginative richness and yet left to him the sting and tang of reality. How vivid in his translation from Villon are those 'eyes with a big gay look out of them would bring folly from a great scholar.' More vivid surely than anything in Swinburne's version, and how noble those words which are yet simple country speech, in which his Petrarch mourns that death came upon Laura just as time was making chastity easy, and the day come when 'lovers may sit together and say out all things are in their hearts,' and 'my sweet enemy was making a start, little by little, to give over her great wariness, the way she was wringing a sweet thing out of my sharp sorrow.'

XIII

Once when I had been saying that though it seemed to me that a conventional descriptive passage encumbered the action at the moment of crisis, I liked The Shadow of the Glen better than Riders to the Sea, that is, for all the nobility of its end, its mood of Greek tragedy, too passive in suffering, and had quoted from Matthew Arnold's introduction to Empedocles on Etna, Synge answered, 'It is a curious thing that The Riders to the Sea succeeds with an English but not with an Irish audience, and The Shadow of the Glen, which is not liked by an English audience, is always liked in Ireland, though it is disliked there in theory.' Since then The Riders to the Sea has grown into great popularity in

Dublin, partly because with the tactical instinct of an Irish mob, the demonstrators against The Playboy both in the press and in the theatre, where it began the evening, selected it for applause. It is now what Shelley's Cloud was for many years a comfort to those who do not like to deny altogether the genius they cannot understand. Yet I am certain that, in the long run, his grotesque plays with their lyric beauty, their violent laughter, The Playboy of the Western World most of all, will be loved for holding so much of the mind of Ireland. Synge has written of The Playboy, 'anyone who has lived in real intimacy with the Irish peasantry will know that the wildest sayings in this play are tame indeed compared with the fancies one may hear at any little hillside cottage of Geesala, or Carraroe, or Dingle Bay.' It is the strangest, the most beautiful expression in drama of that Irish fantasy, which overflowing through all Irish Literature that has come out of Ireland itself (compare the fantastic Irish account of the Battle of Clontarf with the sober Norse account) is the unbroken character of Irish genius. In modern days this genius has delighted in mischievous extravagance, like that of the Gaelic poet's curse upon his children, 'There are three things that I hate, the devil that is waiting for my soul, the worms that are waiting for my body, my children, who are waiting for my wealth and care neither for my body nor my soul: Oh, Christ hang all in the same noose!' I think those words were spoken with a delight in their vehemence that took out of anger half the bitterness with all the gloom. An old man on the Aran Islands told me the very tale on which The Playboy is founded, beginning with the words, 'If any gentleman has done a crime we'll hide him. There was a gentleman that killed his father, and I had him in my own house six months till he got away to America.' Despite the solemnity of his slow speech his eyes shone as the eyes must have shone in that Trinity College branch of the Gaelic League which began every meeting with prayers for the death of an old Fellow of College who disliked their movement, or as they certainly do when patriots are telling how short a time the prayers took to the killing of him. I have seen a crowd, when certain Dublin papers had wrought themselves into an imaginary loyalty, so possessed by what seemed the very genius of satiric fantasy, that one all but looked to find some feathered heel among the cobble stones. Part of the delight of crowd or individual is always that somebody will be angry, somebody take the sport for gloomy earnest. We are mocking at his solemnity, let us therefore so hide our malice that he may be more solemn still, and the laugh run higher yet. Why should we speak his language and so wake him from a dream of all those emotions which men feel because they should, and not because they must? Our minds, being sufficient to themselves, do not wish for victory but are content to elaborate our extravagance, if fortune aid, into wit or lyric beauty, and as for the rest 'There are nights when a king like Conchobar would spit upon his arm-ring and queens will stick out their tongues at the rising moon.' This habit of the mind has made Oscar Wilde and Mr. Bernard Shaw the most celebrated makers of comedy to our time, and if it has sounded plainer still in the conversation of the one, and in some few speeches of the other, that is but because they have not been able to turn out of their plays an alien trick of zeal picked up in struggling youth. Yet, in Synge's plays also, fantasy gives the form and not the thought, for the core is always as in all great art, an over-powering vision of certain virtues, and our capacity for sharing in that vision is the measure of our delight. Great art chills us at first by its coldness or its strangeness, by what seems capricious, and yet it is from these qualities it has authority, as though it had fed on locust and wild honey. The imaginative writer shows us the world as a painter does his picture, reversed in a looking-glass that we may see it, not as it seems to eyes habit has made dull, but as we were Adam and this the first morning; and when the new image becomes as little strange as the old we shall stay with him, because he has, besides, the strangeness, not strange to him, that made us share his vision, sincerity that makes us share his feeling.

To speak of one's emotions without fear or moral ambition, to come out from under the shadow of other men's minds, to forget their needs, to be utterly oneself, that is all the Muses care for. Villon, pander, thief and man-slayer, is as immortal in their eyes, and illustrates in the cry of his ruin as great a truth as Dante in abstract ecstasy, and touches our compassion more. All art is the disengaging of a soul from place and history, its suspension in a beautiful or terrible light, to await the Judgment, and yet, because all its days were a Last Day, judged already. It may show the crimes of Italy as Dante did, or Greek mythology like Keats, or Kerry and Galway villages, and so vividly that ever after I shall look at all with like eyes, and yet I know that Cino da Pistoia thought Dante unjust, that Keats knew no Greek, that those country men and women are neither so lovable nor so lawless as 'mine author sung it me'; that I have added to my being, not my knowledge.

XIV

I wrote the most of these thoughts in my diary on the coast of Normandy, and as I finished came upon Mont Saint Michel, and thereupon doubted for a day the foundation of my school. Here I saw the places of assembly, those cloisters on the rock's summit, the church, the great halls where monks, or knights, or men at arms sat at meals, beautiful from ornament or proportion. I remembered ordinances of the Popes forbidding drinking-cups with stems of gold to these monks who had but a bare dormitory to sleep in. Even when imagining, the individual had taken more from his fellows and his fathers than he gave; one man finishing what another had begun; and all that majestic fantasy, seeming more of Egypt than of Christendom, spoke nothing to the solitary soul, but seemed to announce whether past or yet to come an heroic temper of social men, a bondage of adventure and of wisdom. Then I thought more patiently and I saw that what had made these but as one and given them for a thousand years the miracles of their shrine and temporal rule by land and sea, was not a condescension to knave or dolt, an impoverishment of the common thought to make it serviceable and easy, but a dead language and a communion in whatever, even to the greatest saint, is of incredible difficulty. Only by the substantiation of the soul I thought, whether in literature or in sanctity, can we come upon those agreements, those separations from all else that fasten men together lastingly; for while a popular and picturesque Burns and Scott can but create a province, and our Irish cries and grammars serve some passing need, Homer, Shakespeare, Dante, Goethe and all who travel in their road with however poor a stride define races and create everlasting loyalties. Synge, like all of the great kin, sought for the race, not through the eyes or in history, or even in the future, but where those monks found God, in the depths of the mind, and in all art like his, although it does not command, indeed because it does not, may lie the roots of far-branching events. Only that which does not teach, which does not cry out, which does not persuade, which does not condescend, which does not explain, is irresistible. It is made by men who expressed themselves to the full, and it works through the best minds; whereas the external and picturesque and declamatory writers, that they may create kilts and bagpipes and newspapers and guidebooks, leave the best minds empty, and in Ireland and Scotland, England runs into the hole. It has no array of arguments and maxims, because the great and the simple (and the Muses have never known which of the two most pleases them) need their deliberate thought for the day's work, and yet will do it worse if they have not grown into or found about them, most perhaps in the minds of women, the nobleness of emotion associated with the scenery and events of their country by those great poets who have dreamed it in solitude, and who to this day in Europe are creating indestructible spiritual races, like those religion has created in the East.

September 14th, 1910.

I did not find a word in the printed criticism of Synge's Deirdre of the Sorrows about the qualities that made certain moments seem to me the noblest tragedy, and the play was judged by what seemed to me but wheels and pulleys necessary to the effect, but in themselves nothing.

Upon the other hand, those who spoke to me of the play never spoke of these wheels and pulleys, but if they cared at all for the play, cared for the things I cared for. One's own world of painters, of poets, of good talkers, of ladies who delight in Ricard's portraits or Debussey's music, all those whose senses feel instantly every change in our mother the moon, saw the stage in one way; and those others who look at plays every night, who tell the general playgoer whether this play or that play is to his taste, saw it in a way so different that there is certainly some body of dogma, whether in the instincts or in the memory, pushing the ways apart. A printed criticism, for instance, found but one dramatic moment, that when Deirdre in the second act overhears her lover say that he may grow weary of her; and not one, if I remember rightly, chose for praise or explanation the third act which alone had satisfied the author, or contained in any abundance those sentences that were quoted at the fall of the curtain and for days after.

Deirdre and her lover, as Synge tells the tale, returned to Ireland, though it was nearly certain they would die there, because death was better than broken love, and at the side of the open grave that had been dug for one and would serve for both, quarrelled, losing all they had given their life to keep. 'Is it not a hard thing that we should miss the safety of the grave and we trampling its edge?' That is Deirdre's cry at the outset of a reverie of passion that mounts and mounts till grief itself has carried her beyond grief into pure contemplation. Up to this the play has been a Master's unfinished work, monotonous and melancholy, ill-arranged, little more than a sketch of what it would have grown to, but now I listened breathless to sentences that may never pass away, and as they filled or dwindled in their civility of sorrow, the player, whose art had seemed clumsy and incomplete, like the writing itself, ascended into that tragic ecstasy which is the best that art, perhaps that life, can give. And at last when Deirdre, in the paroxysm before she took her life, touched with compassionate fingers him that had killed her lover, we knew that the player had become, if but for a moment, the creature of that noble mind which had gathered its art in waste islands, and we too were carried beyond time and persons to where passion, living through its thousand purgatorial years, as in the wink of an eye, becomes wisdom; and it was as though we too had touched and felt and seen a disembodied thing.

One dogma of the printed criticism is that if a play does not contain definite character, its constitution is not strong enough for the stage, and that the dramatic moment is always the contest of character with character.

In poetical drama there is, it is held, an antithesis between character and lyric poetry, for lyric poetry, however much it move you when read out of a book, can, as these critics think, but encumber the action. Yet when we go back a few centuries and enter the great periods of drama, character grows less and sometimes disappears, and there is much lyric feeling, and at times a lyric measure will be wrought into the dialogue, a flowing measure that had well-befitted music, or that more lumbering one of the sonnet. Suddenly it strikes us that character is continuously present in comedy alone, and that there is much tragedy, that of Corneille, that of Racine, that of Greece and Rome, where its place is taken by passions and motives, one person being jealous, another full of love or remorse or pride or anger. In writers of tragi-comedy (and Shakespeare is always a writer of tragi-comedy) there is indeed character, but we notice that it is in the moments of comedy that character is defined, in Hamlet's gaiety let us say; while amid the great moments, when Timon orders his tomb, when Hamlet cries to Horatio 'absent thee from felicity awhile,' when Anthony names 'Of many thousand kisses the poor last,' all is lyricism, unmixed passion, 'the integrity of fire.' Nor does character ever attain to complete definition in these lamps ready for the taper, no matter how circumstantial and gradual the opening of events, as it does in Falstaff who has no passionate purpose to fulfill, or as it does in Henry the Fifth whose poetry, never touched by lyric heat, is oratorical; nor when the tragic reverie is at its height do we say, 'How well that man is realised, I should know him were I to meet him in the street,' for it is always ourselves that we see upon the stage, and should it be a tragedy of love we renew, it may be, some loyalty of our youth, and go from the theatre with our eyes dim for an old love's sake.

I think it was while rehearsing a translation of Les Fourberies de Scapin in Dublin, and noticing how passionless it all was, that I saw what should have been plain from the first line I had written, that tragedy must always be a drowning and breaking of the dykes that separate man from man, and that it is upon these dykes comedy keeps house. But I was not certain of the site (one always doubts when one knows no testimony but one's own); till somebody told me of a certain letter of Congreve's. He describes the external and superficial expressions of 'humour' on which farce is founded and then defines 'humour' itself, the foundation of comedy as a 'singular and unavoidable way of doing anything peculiar to one man only, by which his speech and actions are distinguished from all other men,' and adds to it that 'passions are too powerful in the sex to let humour have its course,' or as I would rather put it, that you can find but little of what we call character in unspoiled youth, whatever be the sex, for as he indeed shows in another sentence, it grows with time like the ash of a burning stick, and strengthens towards middle life till there is little else at seventy years.

Since then I have discovered an antagonism between all the old art and our new art of comedy and understand why I hated at nineteen years Thackeray's novels and the new French painting. A big picture of cocottes sitting at little tables outside a café, by some follower of Manet's, was exhibited at the Royal Hibernian Academy while I was a student at a life class there, and I was miserable for days. I found no desirable place, no man I could have wished to be, no woman I could have loved, no Golden Age, no lure for secret hope, no adventure with myself for theme out of that endless tale I told myself all day long. Years after I saw the Olympia of Manet at the Luxembourg and watched it without hostility indeed, but as I might some incomparable talker whose precision of gesture gave me pleasure, though I did not understand his language. I returned to it again and again at intervals of years, saying to myself, 'someday I will understand'; and yet, it was not until Sir Hugh Lane brought the Eva Gonzales to Dublin, and I had said to myself, 'How perfectly that woman is realised as distinct from all other women that have lived or shall live' that I understood I was carrying on in my own mind that quarrel between a tragedian and a comedian which the Devil on Two Sticks in Le Sage showed to the young man who had climbed through the window.

There is an art of the flood, the art of Titian when his Ariosto, and his Bacchus and Ariadne, give new images to the dreams of youth, and of Shakespeare when he shows us Hamlet broken away from life by the passionate hesitations of his reverie. And we call this art poetical, because we must bring more to it than our daily mood if we would take our pleasure; and because it delights in picturing the moment of exaltation, of excitement, of dreaming (or in the capacity for it, as in that still face of Ariosto's that is like some vessel soon to be full of wine). And there is an art that we call real, because character can only express itself perfectly in a real world, being that world's creature, and because we understand it best through a delicate discrimination of the senses which is but entire wakefulness, the daily mood grown cold and crystalline.

We may not find either mood in its purity, but in mainly tragic art one distinguishes devices to exclude or lessen character, to diminish the power of that daily mood, to cheat or blind its too clear perception. If the real world is not altogether rejected, it is but touched here and there, and into the places we have left empty we summon rhythm, balance, pattern, images that remind us of vast passions, the vagueness of past times, all the chimeras that haunt the edge of trance; and if we are painters, we shall express personal emotion through ideal form, a symbolism handled by the generations, a mask from whose eyes the disembodied looks, a style that remembers many masters, that it may escape contemporary suggestion; or we shall leave out some element of reality as in Byzantine painting, where there is no mass, nothing in relief, and so it is that in the supreme moment of tragic art there comes upon one that strange sensation as though the hair of one's head stood up. And when we love, if it be in the excitement of youth, do we not also, that the flood may find no stone to convulse, no wall to narrow it, exclude character or the signs of it by choosing that beauty which seems unearthly because the individual woman is lost amid the labyrinth of its lines as though life were trembling into stillness and silence, or at last folding itself away? Some little irrelevance of line, some promise of character to come, may indeed put us at our ease, 'give more interest' as the humour of the old man with the basket does to Cleopatra's dying; but should it come as we had dreamed in love's frenzy to our dying for that woman's sake, we would find that the discord had its value from the tune.

Nor have we chosen illusion in choosing the outward sign of that moral genius that lives among the subtlety of the passions, and can for her moment make her of the one mind with great artists and poets. In the studio we may indeed say to one another 'character is the only beauty,' but when we choose a wife, as when we go to the gymnasium to be shaped for woman's eyes, we remember academic form, even though we enlarge a little the point of interest and choose "a painter's beauty," finding it the more easy to believe in the fire because it has made ashes.

When we look at the faces of the old tragic paintings, whether it is in Titian or in some painter of medieval China, we find there sadness and gravity, a certain emptiness even, as of a mind that waited the supreme crisis (and indeed it seems at times as if the graphic art, unlike poetry which sings the crisis itself, were the celebration of waiting). Whereas in modern art, whether in Japan or Europe, 'vitality' (is not that the great word of the studios?), the energy, that is to say, which is under the command of our common moments, sings, laughs, chatters or looks its busy thoughts.

Certainly we have here the Tree of Life and that of the knowledge of Good and Evil which is rooted in our interests, and if we have forgotten their differing virtues it is surely because we have taken delight in a confusion of crossing branches. Tragic art, passionate art, the drowner of dykes, the confounder of understanding, moves us by setting us to reverie, by alluring us almost to the intensity of trance. The persons upon the stage, let us say, greaten till they are humanity itself. We feel our minds expand convulsively or spread out slowly like some moon-brightened image-crowded sea. That which is before our eyes perpetually vanishes and returns again in the midst of the excitement it creates, and the more enthralling it is, the more do we forget it.

August, 1910.

JOHN SHAWE-TAYLOR

There is a portrait of John Shawe-Taylor by a celebrated painter in the Dublin Municipal Gallery, but painted in the midst of a movement of the arts that exalts characteristics above the more typical qualities, it does not show us that beautiful and gracious nature. There is an exaggeration of the hollows of the cheeks and of the form of the bones which empties the face of the balance and delicacy of its lines. He was a very handsome man, as women who have imagination and tradition understand those words, and had he not been so, mind and character had been different. There are certain men, certain famous commanders of antiquity, for instance, of whose good looks the historian always speaks, and whose good looks are the image of their faculty; and these men copying hawk or leopard have an energy of swift decision, a power of sudden action, as if their whole body were their brain.

A few years ago he was returning from America, and the liner reached Queenstown in a storm so great that the tender that came out to it for passengers returned with only one man. It was John Shawe-Taylor, who had leaped as it was swept away from the ship.

The achievement that has made his name historic and changed the history of Ireland came from the same faculty of calculation and daring, from that instant decision of the hawk, between the movement of whose wings and the perception of whose eye no time passes capable of division. A proposal for a Land Conference had been made, and cleverer men than he were but talking the life out of it. Every argument for and against had been debated over and over, and it was plain that nothing but argument would come of it. One day we found a letter in the daily papers, signed with his name, saying that a conference would be held on a certain date, and that certain leaders of the landlords and of the tenants were invited. He had made his swift calculation, probably he could not have told the reason for it, a decision had arisen out of his instinct. He was then almost an unknown man. Had the letter failed, he would have seemed a crack-brained fool to his life's end; but the calculation of his genius was justified. He had, as men of his type have often, given an expression to the hidden popular desires; and the expression of the hidden is the daring of the mind. When he had spoken, so many others spoke that the thing was taken out of the mouths of the leaders, it was as though some power deeper than our daily thought had spoken, and men recognised that common instinct, that common sense which is genius. Men like him live near this power because of something simple and impersonal within them which is, as I believe, imaged in the fire of their minds, as in the shape of their bodies and their faces.

I do not think I have known another man whose motives were so entirely pure, so entirely unmixed with any personal calculation, whether of ambition, of prudence or of vanity. He caught up into his imagination the public gain as other men their private gain. For much of his life he had seemed, though a good soldier and a good shot, and a good rider to hounds, to care deeply for nothing but religion, and this religion, so curiously lacking in denominational limits, concerned itself alone with the communion of the soul with God. Such men, before some great decision, will sometimes give to the analysis of their own motive the energy that other men give to the examination of the circumstances wherein they act, and it is often those who attain in this way to purity of motive who act most wisely at moments of great crisis. It is as though they sank a well through the soil where our habits have been built, and where our hopes take root and are again uprooted, to the lasting rock and to the living stream. They are those for whom Tennyson claimed the strength of ten, and the common and clever wonder at their simplicity and at a triumph that has always an air of miracle about it.

Some two years ago Ireland lost a great æsthetic genius, and it may be it should mourn, as it must mourn John Synge always, that which is gone from it in this man's moral genius. And yet it may be that, though he died in early manhood, his work was finished, that the sudden flash of his mind was of those things that come but seldom in a lifetime, and that his name is as much a part of history as though he had lived through many laborious years.

July 1, 1911.

EDMUND SPENSER

I

We know little of Spenser's childhood and nothing of his parents, except that his father was probably an Edmund Spenser of north-east Lancashire, a man of good blood and 'belonging to a house of ancient fame.' He was born in London in 1552, nineteen years after the death of Ariosto, and when Tasso was about eight years old. Full of the spirit of the Renaissance, at once passionate and artificial, looking out upon the world now as craftsman, now as connoisseur, he was to found his art upon theirs rather than upon the more humane, the more noble, the less intellectual art of Malory and the Minstrels. Deafened and blinded by their influence, as so many of us were in boyhood by that art of Hugo, that made the old simple writers seem but as brown bread and water, he was always to love the journey more than its end, the landscape more than the man, and reason more than life, and the tale less than its telling. He entered Pembroke College, Cambridge, in 1569, and translated allegorical poems out of Petrarch and Du Bellay. To-day a young man translates out of Verlaine and Verhaeren; but at that day Ronsard and Du Bellay were the living poets, who promised revolutionary and unheard-of things to a poetry moving towards elaboration and intellect, as ours, the serpent's tooth in his own tail again, moves towards simplicity and instinct. At Cambridge he met with Hobbinol of The Shepheards Calender, a certain Gabriel Harvey, son of a rope-maker at Saffron Walden, but now a Fellow of Pembroke College, a notable man, some five or six years his elder. It is usual to think ill of Harvey because of his dislike of rhyme and his advocacy of classical metres, and because he complained that Spenser preferred his Faerie Queene to the Nine Muses, and encouraged Hobgoblin 'to run off with the Garland of Apollo.' But at that crossroad, where so many crowds mingled talking of so many lands, no one could foretell in what bed he would sleep after nightfall. Milton was in the end to dislike rhyme as much, and it is certain that rhyme is one of the secondary causes of that disintegration of the personal instincts which has given to modern poetry its deep colour for colour's sake, its overflowing pattern, its background of decorative landscape, and its insubordination of detail. At the opening of a movement we are busy with first principles, and can find out everything but the road we are to go, everything but the weight and measure of the impulse, that has come to us out of life itself, for that is always in defiance of reason, always without a justification but by faith and works. Harvey set Spenser to the making of verses in classical metre, and certain lines have come down to us written in what Spenser called 'Iambicum trimetrum.' His biographers agree that they are very bad, but, though I cannot scan them, I find in them the charm of what seems a sincere personal emotion. The man himself, liberated from the minute felicities of phrase and sound, that are the temptation and the delight of rhyme, speaks of his Mistress some thought that came to him not for the sake of poetry, but for love's sake, and the emotion instead of dissolving into detached colours, into 'the spangly gloom' that Keats saw 'froth and boil' when he put his eyes into 'the pillowy cleft,' speaks to her in poignant words as if out of a tear-stained love-letter:

'Unhappie verse, the witnesse of my unhappie state,   Make thy selfe fluttring winge for thy fast flying   Thought, and fly forth to my love wheresoever she be.   Whether lying restlesse in heavy bedde, or else   Sitting so cheerlesse at the cheerful boorde, or else   Playing alone carelesse on her heavenlie virginals.   If in bed, tell hir that my eyes can take no rest;   If at boorde tell her that my mouth can eat no meate   If at her virginals, tell her that I can heare no mirth.'

II

He left College in his twenty-fourth year, and stayed for a while in Lancashire, where he had relations, and there fell in love with one he has written of in The Shepheards Calender as 'Rosalind, the widdowes daughter of the Glenn,' though she was, for all her shepherding, as one learns from a College friend, 'a gentlewoman of no mean house.' She married Menalchus of the Calender and Spenser lamented her for years, in verses so full of disguise that one cannot say if his lamentations come out of a broken heart or are but a useful movement in the elaborate ritual of his poetry, a well-ordered incident in the mythology of his imagination. To no English poet, perhaps to no European poet before his day, had the natural expression of personal feeling been so impossible, the clear vision of the lineaments of human character so difficult; no other's head and eyes had sunk so far into the pillowy cleft. After a year of this life he went to London, and by Harvey's advice and introduction entered the service of the Earl of Leicester, staying for a while in his house on the banks of the Thames; and it was there in all likelihood that he met with the Earl's nephew, Sir Philip Sidney, still little more than a boy, but with his head full of affairs of state. One can imagine that it was the great Earl or Sir Philip Sidney that gave his imagination its moral and practical turn, and one imagines him seeking from philosophical men, who distrust instinct because it disturbs contemplation, and from practical men who distrust everything they cannot use in the routine of immediate events, that impulse and method of creation that can only be learned with surety from the technical criticism of poets, and from the excitement of some movement in the artistic life. Marlowe and Shakespeare were still at school, and Ben Jonson was but five years old. Sidney was doubtless the greatest personal influence that came into Spenser's life, and it was one that exalted moral zeal above every other faculty. The great Earl impressed his imagination very deeply also, for the lamentation over the Earl of Leicester's death is more than a conventional Ode to a dead patron. Spenser's verses about men, nearly always indeed, seem to express more of personal joy and sorrow than those about women, perhaps because he was less deliberately a poet when he spoke of men. At the end of a long beautiful passage he laments that unworthy men should be in the dead Earl's place, and compares them to the fox, an unclean feeder, hiding in the lair 'the badger swept.' The imaginer of the festivals of Kenilworth was indeed the fit patron for him, and alike, because of the strength and weakness of Spenser's art, one regrets that he could not have lived always in that elaborate life, a master of ceremony to the world, instead of being plunged into a life that but stirred him to bitterness, as the way is with theoretical minds in the tumults of events they cannot understand. In the winter of 1579-80 he published The Shepheards Calender, a book of twelve eclogues, one for every month of the year, and dedicated it to Sir Philip Sidney. It was full of pastoral beauty and allegorical images of current events, revealing too that conflict between the æsthetic and moral interests that was to run through well-nigh all his works, and it became immediately famous. He was rewarded with a place as private secretary to the Lord Lieutenant, Lord Grey de Wilton, and sent to Ireland, where he spent nearly all the rest of his life. After a few years there he bought Kilcolman Castle, which had belonged to the rebel Earl of Desmond, and the rivers and hills about this castle came much into his poetry. Our Irish Aubeg is 'Mulla mine, whose waves I taught to weep,' and the Ballyvaughan Hills, it has its rise among 'old Father Mole.' He never pictured the true countenance of Irish scenery, for his mind turned constantly to the courts of Elizabeth and to the umbrageous level lands, where his own race was already seeding like a great poppy:

'Both heaven and heavenly graces do much more   (Quoth he), abound in that same land then this: For there all happie peace and plenteous store   Conspire in one to make contented blisse.   No wayling there nor wretchednesse is heard,   No bloodie issues nor no leprosies,   No griesly famine, nor no raging sweard,   No nightly bordrags, nor no hue and cries;   The shepheards there abroad may safely lie   On hills and downes, withouten dread or daunger,   No ravenous wolves the good mans hope destroy,   Nor outlawes fell affray the forest raunger,   The learned arts do florish in great honor,   And Poets wits are had in peerlesse price.'

Nor did he ever understand the people he lived among or the historical events that were changing all things about him. Lord Grey de Wilton had been recalled almost immediately, but it was his policy, brought over ready-made in his ship, that Spenser advocated throughout all his life, equally in his long prose book The State of Ireland as in the Faerie Queene, where Lord Grey was Artigall and the Iron man the soldiers and executioners by whose hands he worked. Like an hysterical patient he drew a complicated web of inhuman logic out of the bowels of an insufficient premise, there was no right, no law, but that of Elizabeth, and all that opposed her opposed themselves to God, to civilisation, and to all inherited wisdom and courtesy, and should be put to death. He made two visits to England, celebrating one of them in Colin Clouts come Home againe, to publish the first three books and the second three books of the Faerie Queene respectively, and to try for some English office or pension. By the help of Raleigh, now his neighbour at Kilcolman, he had been promised a pension, but was kept out of it by Lord Burleigh, who said, 'All that for a song!' From that day Lord Burleigh became that 'rugged forehead' of the poems, whose censure of this or that is complained of. During the last three or four years of his life in Ireland he married a fair woman of his neighbourhood, and about her wrote many intolerable artificial sonnets and that most beautiful passage in the sixth book of the Faerie Queene, which tells of Colin Clout piping to the Graces and to her; and he celebrated his marriage in the most beautiful of all his poems, the Epithalamium. His genius was pictorial, and these pictures of happiness were more natural to it than any personal pride, or joy, or sorrow. His new happiness was very brief, and just as he was rising to something of Milton's grandeur in the fragment that has been called Mutabilitie, 'the wandering companies that keep the woods,' as he called the Irish armies, drove him to his death. Ireland, where he saw nothing but work for the Iron man, was in the midst of the last struggle of the old Celtic order with England, itself about to turn bottom upward, of the passion of the Middle Ages with the craft of the Renaissance. Seven years after Spenser's arrival in Ireland a large merchant ship had carried off from Loch Swilly, by a very crafty device common in those days, certain persons of importance. Red Hugh, a boy of fifteen, and the coming head of Tirconnell, and various heads of clans had been enticed on board the merchant ship to drink of a fine vintage, and there made prisoners. All but Red Hugh were released, on finding substitutes among the boys of their kindred, and the captives were hurried to Dublin and imprisoned in the Birmingham Tower. After four years of captivity and one attempt that failed, Red Hugh and certain of his companions escaped into the Dublin mountains, one dying there of cold and privation, and from that to their own country-side. Red Hugh allied himself to Hugh O'Neil, the most powerful of the Irish leaders, 'Oh, deep, dissembling heart, born to great weal or woe of thy country!' an English historian had cried to him, an Oxford man too, a man of the Renaissance, and for a few years defeated English armies and shook the power of England. The Irish, stirred by these events, and with it maybe some rumours of The State of Ireland sticking in their stomachs, drove Spenser out of doors and burnt his house, one of his children, as tradition has it, dying in the fire. He fled to England, and died some three months later in January, 1599, as Ben Jonson says, 'of lack of bread.'

During the last four or five years of his life he had seen, without knowing that he saw it, the beginning of the great Elizabethan poetical movement. In 1598 he had pictured the Nine Muses lamenting each one over the evil state in England, of the things that she had in charge, but, like William Blake's more beautiful Whether on Ida's shady brow, their lamentations should have been a cradle-song. When he died Romeo and Juliet, Richard III., and Richard II., and the plays of Marlowe had all been acted, and in stately houses were sung madrigals and love songs whose like has not been in the world since. Italian influence had strengthened the old French joy that had never died out among the upper classes, and an art was being created for the last time in England which had half its beauty from continually suggesting a life hardly less beautiful than itself.

III

When Spenser was buried at Westminster Abbey many poets read verses in his praise, and then threw their verses and the pens that had written them into his tomb. Like him they belonged, for all the moral zeal that was gathering like a London fog, to that indolent, demonstrative Merry England that was about to pass away. Men still wept when they were moved, still dressed themselves in joyous colours, and spoke with many gestures. Thoughts and qualities sometimes come to their perfect expression when they are about to pass away, and Merry England was dying in plays, and in poems, and in strange adventurous men. If one of those poets who threw his copy of verses into the earth that was about to close over his master were to come alive again, he would find some shadow of the life he knew, though not the art he knew, among young men in Paris, and would think that his true country. If he came to England he would find nothing there but the triumph of the Puritan and the merchant, those enemies he had feared and hated, and he would weep perhaps, in that womanish way of his, to think that so much greatness had been, not as he had hoped, the dawn, but the sunset of a people. He had lived in the last days of what we may call the Anglo-French nation, the old feudal nation that had been established when the Norman and the Angevin made French the language of court and market. In the time of Chaucer English poets still wrote much in French, and even English labourers lilted French songs over their work; and I cannot read any Elizabethan poem or romance without feeling the pressure of habits of emotion, and of an order of life which were conscious, for all their Latin gaiety, of a quarrel to the death with that new Anglo-Saxon nation that was arising amid Puritan sermons and Mar-Prelate pamphlets. This nation had driven out the language of its conquerors, and now it was to overthrow their beautiful haughty imagination and their manners, full of abandon and wilfulness, and to set in their stead earnestness and logic and the timidity and reserve of a counting-house. It had been coming for a long while, for it had made the Lollards; and when Anglo-French Chaucer was at Westminster its poet, Langland, sang the office at St. Paul's. Shakespeare, with his delight in great persons, with his indifference to the State, with his scorn of the crowd, with his feudal passion, was of the old nation, and Spenser, though a joyless earnestness had cast shadows upon him, and darkened his intellect wholly at times, was of the old nation too. His Faerie Queene was written in Merry England, but when Bunyan wrote in prison the other great English allegory, Modern England had been born. Bunyan's men would do right that they might come some day to the Delectable Mountain, and not at all that they might live happily in a world whose beauty was but an entanglement about their feet. Religion had denied the sacredness of an earth that commerce was about to corrupt and ravish, but when Spenser lived the earth had still its sheltering sacredness. His religion, where the paganism that is natural to proud and happy people had been strengthened by the platonism of the Renaissance, cherished the beauty of the soul and the beauty of the body with, as it seemed, an equal affection. He would have had men live well, not merely that they might win eternal happiness but that they might live splendidly among men and be celebrated in many songs. How could one live well if one had not the joy of the Creator and of the Giver of gifts? He says in his Hymn to Beauty that a beautiful soul, unless for some stubbornness in the ground, makes for itself a beautiful body, and he even denies that beautiful persons ever lived who had not souls as beautiful. They may have been tempted until they seemed evil, but that was the fault of others. And in his Hymn to Heavenly Beauty he sets a woman little known to theology, one that he names Wisdom or Beauty, above Seraphim and Cherubim and in the very bosom of God, and in the Faerie Queene it is pagan Venus and her lover Adonis who create the forms of all living things and send them out into the world, calling them back again to the gardens of Adonis at their lives' end to rest there, as it seems, two thousand years between life and life. He began in English poetry, despite a temperament that delighted in sensuous beauty alone with perfect delight, that worship of Intellectual Beauty which Shelley carried to a greater subtlety and applied to the whole of life.

The qualities, to each of whom he had planned to give a Knight, he had borrowed from Aristotle and partly Christianised, but not to the forgetting of their heathen birth. The chief of the Knights, who would have combined in himself the qualities of all the others, had Spenser lived to finish the Faerie Queene, was King Arthur, the representative of an ancient quality, Magnificence. Born at the moment of change, Spenser had indeed many Puritan thoughts. It has been recorded that he cut his hair short and half regretted his hymns to Love and Beauty. But he has himself told us that the many-headed beast overthrown and bound by Calidor, Knight of Courtesy, was Puritanism itself. Puritanism, its zeal and its narrowness, and the angry suspicion that it had in common with all movements of the ill-educated, seemed no other to him than a slanderer of all fine things. One doubts, indeed, if he could have persuaded himself that there could be any virtue at all without courtesy, perhaps without something of pageant and eloquence. He was, I think, by nature altogether a man of that old Catholic feudal nation, but, like Sidney, he wanted to justify himself to his new masters. He wrote of knights and ladies, wild creatures imagined by the aristocratic poets of the twelfth century, and perhaps chiefly by English poets who had still the French tongue; but he fastened them with allegorical nails to a big barn door of common sense, of merely practical virtue. Allegory itself had risen into general importance with the rise of the merchant class in the thirteenth and fourteenth centuries; and it was natural when that class was about for the first time to shape an age in its image, that the last epic poet of the old order should mix its art with his own long-descended, irresponsible, happy art.

IV

Allegory and, to a much greater degree, symbolism are a natural language by which the soul when entranced, or even in ordinary sleep, communes with God and with angels. They can speak of things which cannot be spoken of in any other language, but one will always, I think, feel some sense of unreality when they are used to describe things which can be described as well in ordinary words. Dante used allegory to describe visionary things, and the first maker of The Romance of the Rose, for all his lighter spirits, pretends that his adventures came to him in a vision one May morning; while Bunyan, by his preoccupation with heaven and the soul, gives his simple story a visionary strangeness and intensity: he believes so little in the world, that he takes us away from all ordinary standards of probability and makes us believe even in allegory for a while. Spenser, on the other hand, to whom allegory was not, as I think, natural at all, makes us feel again and again that it disappoints and interrupts our preoccupation with the beautiful and sensuous life he has called up before our eyes. It interrupts us most when he copies Langland, and writes in what he believes to be a mood of edification, and the least when he is not quite serious, when he sets before us some procession like a court pageant made to celebrate a wedding or a crowning. One cannot think that he should have occupied himself with moral and religious questions at all. He should have been content to be, as Emerson thought Shakespeare was, a Master of the Revels to mankind. I am certain that he never gets that visionary air which can alone make allegory real, except when he writes out of a feeling for glory and passion. He had no deep moral or religious life. He has never a line like Dante's 'Thy Will is our Peace,' or like Thomas à Kempis's 'The Holy Spirit has liberated me from a multitude of opinions,' or even like Hamlet's objection to the bare bodkin. He had been made a poet by what he had almost learnt to call his sins. If he had not felt it necessary to justify his art to some serious friend, or perhaps even to 'that rugged forehead,' he would have written all his life long, one thinks, of the loves of shepherdesses and shepherds, among whom there would have been perhaps the morals of the dovecot. One is persuaded that his morality is official and impersonal, a system of life which it was his duty to support, and it is perhaps a half understanding of this that has made so many generations believe that he was the first poet laureate, the first salaried moralist among the poets. His processions of deadly sins, and his houses, where the very cornices are arbitrary images of virtue, are an unconscious hypocrisy, an undelighted obedience to the 'rugged forehead,' for all the while he is thinking of nothing but lovers whose bodies are quivering with the memory or the hope of long embraces. When they are not together, he will indeed embroider emblems and images much as those great ladies of the courts of love embroidered them in their castles; and when these are imagined out of a thirst for magnificence and not thought out in a mood of edification, they are beautiful enough; but they are always tapestries for corridors that lead to lovers' meetings or for the walls of marriage chambers. He was not passionate, for the passionate feed their flame in wanderings and absences, when the whole being of the beloved, every little charm of body and of soul, is always present to the mind, filling it with heroical subtleties of desire. He is a poet of the delighted senses, and his song becomes most beautiful when he writes of those islands of Phædria and Acrasia, which angered 'that rugged forehead,' as it seems, but gave to Keats his Belle Dame sans Merci and his 'perilous seas in faery lands forlorn,' and to William Morris his 'waters of the wondrous Isle.'

The dramatists lived in a disorderly world, reproached by many, persecuted even, but following their imagination wherever it led them. Their imagination, driven hither and thither by beauty and sympathy, put on something of the nature of eternity. Their subject was always the soul, the whimsical, self-awakening, self-exciting, self-appeasing soul. They celebrated its heroical, passionate will going by its own path to immortal and invisible things. Spenser, on the other hand, except among those smooth pastoral scenes and lovely effeminate islands that have made him a great poet, tried to be of his time, or rather of the time that was all but at hand. Like Sidney, whose charm it may be led many into slavery, he persuaded himself that we enjoy Virgil because of the virtues of Æneas, and so planned out his immense poem that it would set before the imagination of citizens, in whom there would soon be no great energy, innumerable blameless Æneases. He had learned to put the State, which desires all the abundance for itself, in the place of the Church, and he found it possible to be moved by expedient emotions, merely because they were expedient, and to think serviceable thoughts with no self-contempt. He loved his Queen a little because she was the protectress of poets and an image of that old Anglo-French nation that lay a-dying, but a great deal because she was the image of the State which had taken possession of his conscience. She was over sixty years old, and ugly and, it is thought, selfish, but in his poetry she is 'fair Cynthia,' 'a crown of lilies,' 'the image of the heavens,' 'without mortal blemish,' and has 'an angelic face,' where 'the red rose' has 'meddled with the white'; 'Phoebus thrusts out his golden head' but to look upon her, and blushes to find himself outshone. She is 'a fourth Grace,' 'a queen of love,' 'a sacred saint,' and 'above all her sex that ever yet has been.' In the midst of his praise of his own sweetheart he stops to remember that Elizabeth is more beautiful, and an old man in Daphnaida, although he has been brought to death's door by the death of a beautiful daughter, remembers that though his daughter 'seemed of angelic race,' she was yet but the primrose to the rose beside Elizabeth. Spenser had learned to look to the State not only as the rewarder of virtue but as the maker of right and wrong, and had begun to love and hate as it bid him. The thoughts that we find for ourselves are timid and a little secret, but those modern thoughts that we share with large numbers are confident and very insolent. We have little else to-day, and when we read our newspaper and take up its cry, above all its cry of hatred, we will not think very carefully, for we hear the marching feet. When Spenser wrote of Ireland he wrote as an official, and out of thoughts and emotions that had been organised by the State. He was the first of many Englishmen to see nothing but what he was desired to see. Could he have gone there as a poet merely, he might have found among its poets more wonderful imaginations than even those islands of Phædria and Acrasia. He would have found among wandering story-tellers, not indeed his own power of rich, sustained description, for that belongs to lettered ease, but certainly all the kingdom of Faerie, still unfaded, of which his own poetry was often but a troubled image. He would have found men doing by swift strokes of the imagination much that he was doing with painful intellect, with that imaginative reason that soon was to drive out imagination altogether and for a long time. He would have met with, at his own door, story-tellers among whom the perfection of Greek art was indeed as unknown as his own power of detailed description, but who, none the less, imagined or remembered beautiful incidents and strange, pathetic outcrying that made them of Homer's lineage. Flaubert says somewhere, 'There are things in Hugo, as in Rabelais, that I could have mended, things badly built, but then what thrusts of power beyond the reach of conscious art!' Is not all history but the coming of that conscious art which first makes articulate and then destroys the old wild energy? Spenser, the first poet struck with remorse, the first poet who gave his heart to the State, saw nothing but disorder, where the mouths that have spoken all the fables of the poets had not yet become silent. All about him were shepherds and shepherdesses still living the life that made Theocritus and Virgil think of shepherd and poet as the one thing; but though he dreamed of Virgil's shepherds he wrote a book to advise, among many like things, the harrying of all that followed flocks upon the hills, and of all 'the wandering companies that keep the woods.' His View of the State of Ireland commends indeed the beauty of the hills and woods where they did their shepherding, in that powerful and subtle language of his which I sometimes think more full of youthful energy than even the language of the great playwrights. He is 'sure it is yet a most beautiful and sweet country as any under heaven,' and that all would prosper but for those agitators, 'those wandering companies that keep the woods,' and he would rid it of them by a certain expeditious way. There should be four great garrisons. 'And those fowre garrisons issuing foorthe, at such convenient times as they shall have intelligence or espiall upon the enemye, will so drive him from one side to another and tennis him amongst them, that he shall finde nowhere safe to keepe his creete, or hide himselfe, but flying from the fire shall fall into the water, and out of one daunger into another, that in short space his creete, which is his moste sustenence, shall be wasted in preying, or killed in driving, or starved for wante of pasture in the woodes, and he himselfe brought soe lowe, that he shall have no harte nor abilitye to indure his wretchednesse, the which will surely come to passe in very short space; for one winters well following of him will so plucke him on his knees that he will never be able to stand up agayne.'

He could commend this expeditious way from personal knowledge, and could assure the Queen that the people of the country would soon 'consume themselves and devoure one another. The proofs whereof I saw sufficiently ensampled in these late warres of Mounster; for notwithstanding that the same was a most rich and plentifull countrey, full of corne and cattell, that you would have thought they would have bene able to stand long, yet ere one yeare and a halfe they were brought to such wretchednesse, as that any stonye heart would have rued the same. Out of every corner of the woodes and glynnes they came creeping forth upon theyr hands, for theyr legges could not beare them; they looked like anatomyes of death, they spake like ghosts crying out of their graves; they did eate of the dead carrions, happy were they if they could finde them, yea, and one another soone after, insomuch as the very carcasses they spared not to scrape out of theyr graves; and if they found a plot of watercresses or shamrokes, there they flocked as to a feast for the time, yet not able long to continue therewithall; that in short space there were none allmost left, and a most populous and plentifull countrey suddaynely left voyde of man or beast; yet sure in all that warre, there perished not many by the sword, but all by the extremitye of famine.'

VI

In a few years the Four Masters were to write the history of that time, and they were to record the goodness or the badness of Irishman and Englishman with entire impartiality. They had seen friends and relatives persecuted, but they would write of that man's poisoning and this man's charities and of the fall of great houses, and hardly with any other emotion than a thought of the pitiableness of all life. Friend and enemy would be for them a part of the spectacle of the world. They remembered indeed those Anglo-French invaders who conquered for the sake of their own strong hand, and when they had conquered became a part of the life about them, singing its songs, when they grew weary of their own Iseult and Guinevere. The Four Masters had not come to understand, as I think, despite famines and exterminations, that new invaders were among them, who fought for an alien State, for an alien religion. Such ideas were difficult to them, for they belonged to the old individual, poetical life, and spoke a language even, in which it was all but impossible to think an abstract thought. They understood Spain, doubtless, which persecuted in the interests of religion, but I doubt if anybody in Ireland could have understood as yet that the Anglo-Saxon nation was beginning to persecute in the service of ideas it believed to be the foundation of the State. I doubt if anybody in Ireland saw that with certainty, till the Great Demagogue had come and turned the old house of the noble into 'the house of the Poor, the lonely house, the accursed house of Cromwell.' He came, another Cairbry Cat Head, with that great rabble, who had overthrown the pageantry of Church and Court, but who turned towards him faces full of the sadness and docility of their long servitude, and the old individual, poetical life went down, as it seems, forever. He had studied Spenser's book and approved of it, as we know, finding, doubtless, his own head there, for Spenser, a king of the old race, carried a mirror which showed kings yet to come though but kings of the mob. Those Bohemian poets of the theatres were wiser, for the States that touched them nearly were the States where Helen and Dido had sorrowed, and so their mirrors showed none but beautiful heroical heads. They wandered in the places that pale passion loves, and were happy, as one thinks, and troubled little about those marching and hoarse-throated thoughts that the State has in its pay. They knew that those marchers, with the dust of so many roads upon them, are very robust and have great and well-paid generals to write expedient despatches in sound prose; and they could hear mother earth singing among her cornfields:

'Weep not, my wanton! smile upon my knee;   When thou art old there's grief enough for thee.'

VII

There are moments when one can read neither Milton nor Spenser, moments when one recollects nothing but that their flesh had partly been changed to stone, but there are other moments when one recollects nothing but those habits of emotion that made the lesser poet especially a man of an older, more imaginative time. One remembers that he delighted in smooth pastoral places, because men could be busy there or gather together there, after their work, that he could love handiwork and the hum of voices. One remembers that he could still rejoice in the trees, not because they were images of loneliness and meditation, but because of their serviceableness. He could praise 'the builder oake,' 'the aspine, good for staves,' 'the cypresse funerall,' 'the eugh, obedient to the bender's will,' 'the birch for shaftes,' 'the sallow for the mill,' 'the mirrhe sweete-bleeding in the bitter wound,' 'the fruitful olive,' and 'the carver holme.' He was of a time before undelighted labour had made the business of men a desecration. He carries one's memory back to Virgil's and Chaucer's praise of trees, and to the sweet-sounding song made by the old Irish poet in their praise.

I got up from reading the Faerie Queene the other day and wandered into another room. It was in a friend's house, and I came of a sudden to the ancient poetry and to our poetry side by side, an engraving of Claude's 'Mill' hung under an engraving of Turner's 'Temple of Jupiter.' Those dancing country-people, those cow-herds, resting after the day's work, and that quiet mill-race made one think of Merry England with its glad Latin heart, of a time when men in every land found poetry and imagination in one another's company and in the day's labour. Those stately goddesses, moving in slow procession towards that marble architrave among mysterious trees, belong to Shelley's thought, and to the religion of the wilderness, the only religion possible to poetry to-day. Certainly Colin Clout, the companionable shepherd, and Calidor, the courtly man-at-arms, are gone, and Alastor is wandering from lonely river to river finding happiness in nothing but in that star where Spenser too had imagined the fountain of perfect things. This new beauty, in losing so much, has indeed found a new loftiness, a something of religious exaltation that the old had not. It may be that those goddesses, moving with a majesty like a procession of the stars, mean something to the soul of man that those kindly women of the old poets did not mean, for all the fulness of their breasts and the joyous gravity of their eyes. Has not the wilderness been at all times a place of prophecy?

VIII

Our poetry, though it has been a deliberate bringing back of the Latin joy and the Latin love of beauty, has had to put off the old marching rhythms, that once delighted more than expedient hearts, in separating itself from a life where servile hands have become powerful. It has ceased to have any burden for marching shoulders, since it learned ecstasy from Smart in his mad cell, and from Blake, who made joyous little songs out of almost unintelligible visions, and from Keats, who sang of a beauty so wholly preoccupied with itself that its contemplation is a kind of lingering trance.

The poet, if he would not carry burdens that are not his and obey the orders of servile lips, must sit apart in contemplative indolence playing with fragile things.

If one chooses at hazard a Spenserian stanza out of Shelley and compares it with any stanza by Spenser, one sees the change, though it would be still more clear if one had chosen a lyrical passage. I will take a stanza out of Laon and Cythna, for that is story-telling and runs nearer to Spenser than the meditative Adonais:

'The meteor to its far morass returned: The beating of our veins one interval Made still; and then I felt the blood that burned Within her frame, mingle with mine, and fall Around my heart like fire; and over all A mist was spread, the sickness of a deep And speechless swoon of joy, as might befall Two disunited spirits when they leap In union from this earth's obscure and fading sleep.

The rhythm is varied and troubled, and the lines, which are in Spenser like bars of gold thrown ringing one upon another, are broken capriciously. Nor is the meaning the less an inspiration of indolent muses, for it wanders hither and thither at the beckoning of fancy. It is now busy with a meteor and now with throbbing blood that is fire, and with a mist that is a swoon and a sleep that is life. It is bound together by the vaguest suggestion, while Spenser's verse is always rushing on to some preordained thought. 'A popular poet' can still indeed write poetry of the will, just as factory girls wear the fashion of hat or dress the moneyed classes wore a year ago, but 'popular poetry' does not belong to the living imagination of the world. Old writers gave men four temperaments, and they gave the sanguineous temperament to men of active life, and it is precisely the sanguineous temperament that is fading out of poetry and most obviously out of what is most subtle and living in poetry, its pulse and breath, its rhythm. Because poetry belongs to that element in every race which is most strong, and therefore most individual, the poet is not stirred to imaginative activity by a life which is surrendering its freedom to ever new elaboration, organisation, mechanism. He has no longer a poetical will, and must be content to write out of those parts of himself which are too delicate and fiery for any deadening exercise. Every generation has more and more loosened the rhythm, more and more broken up and disorganised, for the sake of subtlety of detail, those great rhythms which move, as it were, in masses of sound. Poetry has become more spiritual, for the soul is of all things the most delicately organised, but it has lost in weight and measure and in its power of telling long stories and of dealing with great and complicated events. Laon and Cythna, though I think it rises sometimes into loftier air than the Faerie Queene; and Endymion, though its shepherds and wandering divinities have a stranger and more intense beauty than Spenser's, have need of too watchful and minute attention for such lengthy poems. In William Morris, indeed, one finds a music smooth and unexacting like that of the old story-tellers, but not their energetic pleasure, their rhythmical wills. One too often misses in his Earthly Paradise the minute ecstasy of modern song without finding that old happy-go-lucky tune that had kept the story marching.

Spenser's contemporaries, writing lyrics or plays full of lyrical moments, write a verse more delicately organised than his and crowd more meaning into a phrase than he, but they could not have kept one's attention through so long a poem. A friend who has a fine ear told me the other day that she had read all Spenser with delight and yet could remember only four lines. When she repeated them they were from the poem by Matthew Roydon, which is bound up with Spenser because it is a commendation of Sir Philip Sidney:

'A sweet, attractive kind of grace, A full assurance given by looks, Continual comfort in a face, The lineaments of Gospel books.'

Yet if one were to put even these lines beside a fine modern song one would notice that they had a stronger and rougher energy, a featherweight more, if eye and ear were fine enough to notice it, of the active will, of the happiness that comes out of life itself.

IX

I have put into this book[5] only those passages from Spenser that I want to remember and carry about with me. I have not tried to select what people call characteristic passages, for that is, I think, the way to make a dull book. One never really knows anybody's taste but one's own, and if one likes anything sincerely one may be certain that there are other people made out of the same earth to like it too. I have taken out of The Shepheards Calender only those parts which are about love or about old age, and I have taken out of the Faerie Queene passages about shepherds and lovers, and fauns and satyrs, and a few allegorical processions. I find that though I love symbolism, which is often the only fitting speech for some mystery of disembodied life, I am for the most part bored by allegory, which is made, as Blake says, 'by the daughters of memory,' and coldly, with no wizard frenzy. The processions I have chosen are either those, like the House of Mammon, that have enough ancient mythology, always an implicit symbolism, or, like the Cave of Despair, enough sheer passion to make one forget or forgive their allegory, or else they are, like that vision of Scudamour, so visionary, so full of a sort of ghostly midnight animation, that one is persuaded that they had some strange purpose and did truly appear in just that way to some mind worn out with war and trouble. The vision of Scudamour is, I sometimes think, the finest invention in Spenser. Until quite lately I knew nothing of Spenser but the parts I had read as a boy. I did not know that I had read so far as that vision, but year after year this thought would rise up before me coming from I knew not where. I would be alone perhaps in some old building, and I would think suddenly 'out of that door might come a procession of strange people doing mysterious things with tumult. They would walk over the stone floor, then suddenly vanish, and everything would become silent again.' Once I saw what is called, I think, a Board School continuation class play Hamlet. There was no stage, but they walked in procession into the midst of a large room full of visitors and of their friends. While they were walking in, that thought came to me again from I knew not where. I was alone in a great church watching ghostly kings and queens setting out upon their unearthly business.

It was only last summer, when I read the Fourth Book of the Faerie Queene, that I found I had been imagining over and over the enchanted persecution of Amoret.

I give too, in a section which I call 'Gardens of Delight,' the good gardens of Adonis and the bad gardens of Phædria and Acrasia, which are mythological and symbolical, but not allegorical, and show, more particularly those bad islands, his power of describing bodily happiness and bodily beauty at its greatest. He seemed always to feel through the eyes, imagining everything in pictures. Marlowe's Hero and Leander is more energetic in its sensuality, more complicated in its intellectual energy than this languid story, which pictures always a happiness that would perish if the desire to which it offers so many roses lost its indolence and its softness. There is no passion in the pleasure he has set amid perilous seas, for he would have us understand that there alone could the war-worn and the sea-worn man find dateless leisure and unrepining peace.

October, 1902.

Footnotes:

[1] I had forgotten Falstaff, who is an episode in a chronicle play.

[2] Rose Kavanagh, the poet, wrote to her religious adviser from, I think, Leitrim, where she lived, and asked him to get her the works of Mazzini. He replied, 'You must mean Manzone.'

[3] I have heard him say more than once, 'I will not say our people know good from bad, but I will say that they don't hate the good when it is pointed out to them, as a great many people do in England.'

[4] A small political organiser told me once that he and a certain friend got together somewhere in Tipperary a great meeting of farmers for O'Leary on his coming out of prison, and O'Leary had said at it: 'The landlords gave us some few leaders, and I like them for that, and the artisans have given us great numbers of good patriots, and so I like them best: but you I do not like at all, for you have never given us anyone.' I have known but one that had his moral courage, and that was a woman with beauty to give her courage and self-possession.

[5] Poems of Spenser: Selected and with an Introduction by W. B. Yeats. (T. C. and E. C. Jack, Edinburgh, N.D.)

William Butler Yeats – A Short Biography

William Butler Yeats (1865 – 1939) is best described as Ireland's national poet in addition to being one of the major twentieth-century literary figures of the English tongue. To many literary critics, Yeats represents the 'Romantic poet of modernism,' which is quite revealing about his extraordinary style that combines between the outward emphasis on the expression of emotions and the extensive use of symbolism, imagery and allusions. Yeats also wrote prose and drama and established himself as the spokesman of the Irish cause. His fame was greatly boosted mainly after he received the Nobel Prize in Literature in 1923. His life was marked by his many love stories, by his great interest in oriental mysticism and occultism as well as by political engagement since he served as an Irish senator for two terms. Today, although William Butler Yeats's contribution to literary modernism and to Irish nationalism remains incontestable, his poetic oeuvre represents his finest achievement and will always be part and parcel of the English poetic canon.

William Butler Yeats was born in the year 1865 in the Irish capital Dublin to be raised by a family that historically had a passion for the arts. Young Yeats received his earlier education at home before the family moved to London where he never forgot his passion for Irish Gaelic culture, language, and mythology. The latter were to haunt him throughout his whole life and to find their way to his most acknowledged verse. One may venture to say that Yeats inherited the poetic and Romantic talents of such poets as Edmund Spencer, John Donne, Percy Bysshe Shelley, and William Blake while adding to his verse a flavor of Irish lore. Yeats was only two years when the family settled in London. This was mainly in order to enable his elder siblings to pursue their artistic careers. In addition to the formal education that he received at the Godolphin School, Yeats was continuously instructed by his mother and by his brother John who focused mainly on experimental sciences.
The family's stay in London was interrupted, though. They had to return to Dublin in the early 1880s where the teenage Irish man attended Erasmus Smith High School and then the National College of Art and Design. They remained there until 1887 when they went back to London anew. It was during those years that Yeats, while making acquaintances with a

number of writers and painters, started to arrange his earliest poetic lines. A number of prose writings and poems were published in the *Dublin University Review*. Later, some Irish publication houses started to publish Yeats's works which combined between verse and prose. For instance, in 1886 Yeats combined between poetry and drama in the play *Mosada* while two years later he published a volume entitled Fairy and Folk Tales of the Irish Peasantry. His first poetic volume was published in 1889 under the title *The Wanderings of Oisin and Other Poems*. Many readers and critics agree that Yeats's early writings were particularly influenced by Shelley, Spencer and then William Blake. The presence of Irish mythology and folklore is to fade away in the later phase of his career.

In 1890, while publishing one of his most successful and acknowledged poems entitled "The Lake Isle of Innisfree," Yeats launched a poetry club with a group of fellow poets that used to meet at a local tavern to exchange ideas and recitals of their modernist poetry. The group was given the name "The Rhymers' Club" and had achieved a considerable reputation in London. By the 1890s, Yeats started to produce profuse and diversified writings. These included, but were not limited to, *Irish Faerie Tales* (1892), *The Countess Kathleen and Various Legends and Lyrics* (1892), a play entitled *The land of Heart's Desire* (1894) and more than one volume of short stories and poetry. Yeats continuously combined between poetry, fiction and drama. He wrote drama in verse as well as narrative poetry drawing on mythology and popular folktales.

Yeats remained very prolific during the rest of his life. In the 1900s, more poetry volumes and plays followed as well as non-fictional writings in the style of philosophical reflections and spiritual contemplations such as *Ideas of Good and Evil* (1903) and Discoveries (1907). While the second phase of Yeats's career as a poet was conventionally marked by his gradual detachment from the classic and the Romantic schools, it showed his great interest in oriental mysticism, spiritualism and occultism. The poet was seriously concerned with this esoteric world that he wanted to explore and fully understand. While being influenced by the works of the Swedish theologian and mystic Emanuel Swedenborg, Yeats took part in different clubs and associations that were interested in the paranormal. He and his fellow organized séances and claimed that they interacted with ghosts and spirits. By and large, critics and biographers maintain divergent views on the impact of such interest on the value and merits of the poet's oeuvre. Some harshly criticize Yeats and dismiss his interest in the occult as "nonsense" and some believe that it represents a serious and respectable exploration of the dark and unmapped world of the metaphysical.

Earlier in 1899, Yeats's passion for theatre made him found with a number of fellow playwrights and intellectuals the Abbey Theatre, or The National Theatre of Ireland in the city of Dublin. This enabled him to perform his own experimental plays as well as plays by others that sought to establish an Irish theatrical tradition.

In the 1910s, Yeats's style became more sophisticated and his style reached an unprecedented degree of beauty and refinement. This manifests itself in poems such as "Easter, 1916" published in the eponymous year and "The Wild Swans at Coole" first published in 1917, then revised in 1919. In 1920, Yeats published what many still consider as his most brilliant poetic achievement under the title "The Second Coming." The style of Yeats's later poems was marked by the heavy use of symbolism and imagery in addition to its respect of rhyme and meter. Yeats mainly developed a tendency towards the extensive use of illusions. References to glorious and dignified events, places and characters such as the Trojan wars, Byzantium, Greek and Christian mythologies are frequent in his verse and led to a revival of this old tradition in the modern epoch. Most critics distinguish between Yeats and his contemporaries and personal friends Ezra Pound and T. S. Eliot, regarding the first as representing a traditionalist tendency among the modernist.

Moreover, it is seldom enough to insist on Yeats's spiritual and mystic side which was greatly reflected in his later writings. Yeats's exploration of the spiritual world and the nature of the divine and the soul was a life-time quest and while leaving its traces in most of his remarkable works, it culminated in the publication of *A Vision* in 1925. Other successful works that appeared in Yeats's later years included his play *The Resurrection* (1927) and the volume of poetry entitled *The Tow*er (1928) which included the very famous "Sailing to Byzantium." Interestingly, Yeats continued writing until his last days and the most important achievement of his final years was probably *The Winding Stair and Other Poems* published in 1933.

Being a rather romantic gentleman and obviously a handsome man, women had a special impact on Yeats's life as well as on his literary works. His name and reputation were mainly associated with one woman that he had supposedly loved throughout his whole life, Maud Gonne. The latter was a beautiful lady much concerned with the cause of Irish nationalism. Yeats was so infatuated with Gonne that he repeatedly proposed to her, but in vain. Apparently, the poet was not ardent enough to please the young lady who felt much more committed to her cause than to him. She married the Irish nationalist Major John MacBride instead. The friendship of the couple persisted, though, and she maintained her status as an inspirational muse for the poet all along his career.

Nevertheless, Yeats was an Irish nationalist too. He was probably just less convinced of pure militancy and was more inclined towards artistic resistance. It is equally noteworthy that Yeats belonged to the Protestant minority in Ireland and had a very critical stance on the Catholicism of the majority. He seemingly hated the general association of Irish nationalism with the Catholic Church as a symbol of national identity and distinction from the English, an association that Gonne was drawn to. These details did never alienate the poet from his sense of nationalism which was later reconfirmed when he was hailed by the Nobel Prize committee as the poet of the Irish nation. Yeats's nationalism was also recognized by his native country when he was appointed to the first Irish Senate in 1922 and then in 1925. In addition to Maud Gonne, Yeats also knew other women from the intellectual and artistic circles that he frequented, most of whom are way younger than him. These included Olivia Shakespear and Georgie Hyde Lees who became his wife in 1917.

In 1928, Yeats started to have serious health problems and was forced to leave the Senate. Yet, he soon recovered, mainly after undergoing an operation in 1934. He spent the remaining years of his existence publishing prolifically and having more romantic affairs with younger women. He also edited and published anthologies of modern poetry that were to mark those extraordinary decades of the twentieth century. It was on January 28th, 1939 that William Butler Yeats died in Menton, France. Following his personal wish, he was first buried in the French town of Roquebrune-Cap-Martin to be later moved and re-interred at Drumcliff, County Sligo in Ireland where he spent some of his childhood years.